AMISH TULIP

AMISH LOVE BLOOMS BOOK 2

SAMANTHA PRICE

AMISH ROMANCE

CHAPTER 1

*N*ancy Yoder had been successful in getting her oldest daughter, Rose, married in a timely fashion. Organizing people and events was what Nancy did best, and with her encouragement, Rose had finally seen the sense in getting married young. With the wedding held at their house now coming to a close, Nancy leaned against the outside wall, feeling a deep sense of satisfaction. The guests were just finishing the main meal, and the desserts were ready to be distributed —a perfect time to have a break.

Now that they were married, Rose and Mark would be moving into a small house on Mark's uncle's land, which left only the twins and Tulip still in the family home. Once they were all off her hands, Nancy figured she would take life easier and enjoy some time alone with her husband, Hezekiah. Of course, there would be the added benefit of the grandchildren that would follow the marriages and she was looking forward to watching them arrive. Her oldest son and his wife had already had a daughter and she'd been a blessing to the whole family. It was high time for her second eldest son who'd been married for more than a year to give her a grandchild.

Nancy looked around for Tulip, her next project. Squinting hard, Nancy saw that her daughter was at the far end of the yard speaking with three young men. Wasting no time, she hurried over to find out exactly who these young men were. As she drew closer, she noticed that only one man looked familiar and she didn't recognize the other two.

Tulip glanced at her mother as she approached and didn't look happy to see her. Nancy knew Tulip didn't like her knowing too much about her friends. She'd developed a habit of being far too private and that didn't suit Nancy one little bit.

"*Mamm!* Do you want me to help with the food again?"

"It's a bit late for that, Tulip. Why don't you introduce me to your friends?"

"*Jah,* okay. Sorry. *Mamm,* this is Andrew, and this is Nathanial, and of course you know Phillip." She turned to the young men and almost as an apology said, "This is my *mudder,* Nancy Yoder."

"Hello, Mrs. Yoder," one of the young men said, while the other two nodded politely.

"And where are you all from?" Nancy swept her gaze across the three of them. As they talked, she found out that one young man was from Oakes County, another was from their community, and the third one of them belonged to people from Ohio. It was all too much for her to remember, the three names let alone where each of them was from. She told herself she'd find out more from

Tulip later in the night and whether Tulip might be interested in one of them in particular. Her job of finding Tulip a husband might well be easier than she thought it would be, but only if Tulip didn't carry on in the ridiculous secretive manner she'd had of late.

"Are you going to say hello to Aunt Nerida, *Mamm?* It looks like she's leaving," Tulip said, staring at the row of buggies.

Nancy glanced over at her only sister, who she didn't get along with. Tulip was simply trying to get rid of her mother, Nancy knew that, but she kept staring at Nerida and her two daughters, surprised they'd bothered to come at all. They hadn't made any effort to come to either of her son's weddings. Not wanting to create a bad example to Tulip, she said, "*Jah,* I suppose I should thank her for coming and be cordial."

After she had nodded a goodbye to the young men, Nancy strode toward her sister. If Nerida really wanted to make amends with her, she would've stepped up and helped with the food. And if that wasn't the reason she'd come, then what was the reason? Perhaps Nerida and her girls were hungry and had come for the food? Nancy amused herself with that thought.

Nerida and she had been the only girls, with ten older brothers, and Nancy was a year older. The thing that had forever irritated Nancy was that her younger sister had a bad habit of copying everything she did. And Nerida knew that her copying had always bothered Nancy. The worst thing and the most unforgiveable thing Nerida had done was to steal Nancy's idea of calling her daughters names of flowers. That was *her* thing—her theme for the girls, and her sister should've known that she shouldn't have copied. Nerida had called her first child Violet, and her second, Willow. When Nancy had confronted her about it, Nerida called her ridiculous and told her that 'Willow' wasn't even a flower. She'd acted like Nancy was making a fuss over nothing. The name Willow was close enough to Nancy's thinking, and from that moment, a rift developed between the sisters.

"Are you leaving already, Nerida?"

Nerida was already in the driver's seat of the buggy. She took hold of the reins before she looked at Nancy.

"Hello, Aunt Nancy," the two girls chorused from the buggy.

"Hello, Violet and Willow." She smiled at her pretty nieces who were both a little younger than Nancy's twins. "I haven't seen you all for some time."

"And whose fault is that?" Nerida quipped.

"Mamm!" Violet, the older of the girls looked shocked at the way her mother had spoken.

"Why don't you stay on a little so we can talk?" Nancy suggested to Nerida, After all, weddings were about families. Nerida's presence signaled a step to reconciliation, so Nancy was also taking a step.

Nerida tilted her chin high and said down the end of her nose, "I'm only here for Rose. She's a sweet girl, and the girls wanted to come to the wedding too."

"We love weddings," Willow said.

"We're just serving the dessert," Nancy said, hoping that would make at least the girls want to stay on. "Wouldn't you girls like to stay longer?"

"It's not their decision, Nancy."

"Couldn't we stay, *Mamm?*" Violet asked.

Willow added from the backseat of the buggy, "Just a little longer?"

"*Nee.* Goodbye, Nancy." Nerida slapped the reins against the horse's neck, and the horse walked forward.

Nancy stood and watched the buggy leave. They were the first guests to leave the wedding. *Well, Hezekiah can't say that I didn't try.*

CHAPTER 2

When Nancy was standing back by the house, Rose and Nancy's eyes met and Rose gave her mother a little wave. Nancy smiled and waved back at her newly married daughter.

"Well, we've got three married off and three to go."

Nancy jumped at the sound of her husband's deep voice. She hadn't noticed him walking up behind her. "There you are. I was just thinking the very same thing. With the boys and Rose married now, there are only Tulip and the twins to go. Then we'll be alone again—at last. That will be the best outcome." Nancy giggled.

Hezekiah chuckled along with her. "Don't forget all the *grosskinner* we'll have."

"I'm not forgetting about that, or our little Shirley. She's been a blessing for the whole *familye.* She needs other children to play with; that's something I think about every day."

"There are plenty of children she can play with."

Hezekiah put a hand gently on his wife's shoulder. "That will all happen in time, Nancy, all in *Gott's* timing."

Nancy nodded and then her husband walked away. Hezekiah thought that things happened by themselves under God's general oversight, and she wasn't about to disagree with him, but sometimes God used people's actions to fulfill His will. That's all Nancy was doing; she was being God's helper to get her three remaining daughters married and off her hands.

Tulip was smart, so she needed a man equally smart, but where would she go to find one of those? Nancy looked around the crowd. It was getting harder just to find a single man, as many of them had married over the past year.

Seeing Tulip still talking with the same three young men, she decided to invite them all to Tulip's birthday. She left Hezekiah standing there and hurried back to Tulip's side. "It's your birthday soon and we always have a big party for you."

"That's not necessary, *Mamm.* I'm not interested in birthdays, not mine, anyway. I don't like a lot of fuss."

Nancy shook her head. "That's nonsense." She turned to the three young men. "I hope all of you will be able to come?"

"We would love to," one of them said. "At least, I'll be there. What day is it?"

"Wednesday upcoming."

"We'll be there," another of the men said, as the other two smiled.

Nancy was pleased that the three men appeared delighted to be invited. *"Gut!* Shall we say seven o'clock?"

All the boys nodded in agreement.

"If you'll excuse me, there are some other people I need to organize for serving the desserts." Nancy walked away, pleased with herself, and then hurried to find some more single men to invite to Tulip's birthday. Weddings were the best places for young men and women to gather, and they brought in many visitors from other communities far and wide. Tulip was stuck speaking to the same three men, so Nancy would have to do the legwork for her. She could not let this opportunity pass her by.

Nancy organized the serving of the desserts and then spent the next hour meeting as many young men as she could. She invited every one she could to her daughter's birthday.

TULIP WAS glad that her mother hadn't caught on to the fact that one of the boys she'd been speaking with was Jacob Schumacher's brother, Nathanial. Jacob had disappointed her sister, Rose, several months ago before she married, and then he left their community to go back to Oakes County to marry someone else. Jacob had gotten a young woman into a situation where they *had* to marry. Of course, none of that was Nathanial's fault, but her mother was stubborn and would fail to see it that way. Things turned out much better for Rose because the hurt from Jacob's deception opened her eyes to Mark, who had loved her since they were young. Rose and Mark were a far better match than Rose and Jacob would've ever been.

Now Tulip and Nathanial were alone, since the other

two young men were talking with others nearby. Nathanial was a handsome man, much like his brother, Jacob. His hair was rich brown in color, and his eyes were a vivid blue-green that stood out against his tanned olive skin. He was so handsome that Tulip could barely take her eyes from him.

"I might stay on a few weeks more."

"That would be nice. Can you do that? What about your job?" Tulip asked.

"I'm in between jobs at the moment. I'm told there could be work around here."

Tulip smiled. She knew Nathanial liked her by the way he continually smiled and hung around making conversation. If she married him things could be awkward because Rose would be even more closely related—by two marriages—to Jacob, since Jacob was Mark's cousin.

"Your *schweschder* looks happy," he said, looking over at the wedding table at the end of the Yoder's yard.

Tulip glanced over at Rose. "She is. She's in love with Mark. He's always loved her."

"And what about you?"

She stared at him. "Me?"

"*Jah,* do you have a man in your life?"

"*Nee,* I don't right now." She giggled and looked down at her lace-up boots. The complete truth was that Tulip had never had a man in her life.

"Can I see you sometime? Alone, I mean."

She looked into his blue-green eyes and her heart gave a flutter. "I'd like that."

"I'm staying with my aunt and uncle, Mark and Matthew's parents." He nodded toward her house. "I already know where you live. Maybe I can see you before your birthday?"

Tulip nodded, wondering what her mother would say if she learned that she'd accidently invited Jacob's brother to her birthday. "Okay. What did you have in mind?"

"Can I see you—maybe Saturday afternoon? Can you get away and head into town?"

"I'll try."

"We could meet at Little Beans Café. It's a nice place. I went there yesterday with Matthew."

"I know where it is. What time?"

"Two?"

"I think I could do that." The only way she would be able to get away was to tell her mother she was meeting friends in town. She couldn't tell her she was meeting Jacob's brother. If she did, her mother wouldn't allow it, or worse, she'd send her younger twin sisters with her. That would completely ruin all her chances with him. The twins would tell stories to Nathanial and make Tulip look a fool. Either choice would be a complete disaster. She didn't like lying, so she hoped her mother wouldn't probe too far into where she was going on Saturday.

He smiled at her. "I'm looking forward to it."

"Me too." She glanced down at her boots and then looked back up at his handsome face. "I should see if *Mamm* needs my help."

He nodded. "I'll see you on Saturday."

"Okay." Tulip walked away as though she were floating. She pushed some loose strands of dark hair back under her *kapp* as she walked between rows of tables. The second seating of the meal had taken place and now the women were running the desserts out from the kitchen.

As soon as she walked into the house, a line of women with their arms full of either serving trays or bowls passed her. In the kitchen, her mother barked out orders at her. She too took several trips out with large serving bowls and trays of desserts to place on the tables.

When Tulip placed the last of the desserts down on one of the tables, she looked around at the hundreds of guests, most of whom were seated. She no longer felt hungry because of Nathanial. Not only had he made her feel light-headed, he'd taken her appetite away. She looked around for him and spotted him eating at a table next to his cousin, Matthew. He caught her eye and smiled at her. It was as though they had a secret that was their very own.

She turned around to see her father and the twins at the table in front of her, so she sat with them. Even though she wasn't hungry, she helped herself to a large piece of apple pie and spooned on a large helping of cream. If she sat there without eating, her twin sisters would say something about it and tease her. Tulip wasn't in the mood.

"It'll be you next, Tulip," Daisy, one of her sisters, said.

Tulip knew what she was teasing her about. It was time to do a little teasing of her own. *"Nee,* I think it will be both of you. *Mamm's* writing to all the communities and finding twin boys your age, or a little older, for you to marry."

"Is she?" Lily's face lit up like a lantern on a dark winter's night.

Their father chuckled. "Your *schweschder's* only having fun with you."

Daisy frowned at her. "*Jah,* having fun at my expense is what she's doing. How could you be so mean, Tulip? It sounds just like something *Mamm* would do."

"*Jah,* that would be *gut,* to marry twins, wouldn't it, Daisy?" Lily asked. "Then we could all live in one big *haus.*"

"And each have twin *bopplis,*" Daisy added with a giggle. "Three sets of twins each."

Lily added, "They can be the same ages so they can grow up together."

Tulip pulled a face. Did the world need more twins like her sisters? Tulip said, full of sarcasm, "Would you ever consider marrying someone who wasn't a twin?"

"*Nee,*" both of them said at once.

"I don't think that'll happen. I haven't heard of twin boys your age," their father said as he helped himself to more dessert.

Lily said, "Don't be like that, *Dat.* You have to believe there are some out there somewhere."

Their father chuckled again. "You never know, but I would be surprised if that happened, so don't wait for these twins."

"I've found a man for you, Tulip."

Tulip leaned forward, not knowing whether Daisy was being serious or silly. "Where is he?"

"Over there."

She turned and looked where her sister was pointing to see Jonathon Byler, a quiet single man in his late twenties. He was very much overweight. Tulip wouldn't let on she knew they were teasing her and being mean about Jonathon. It would only draw attention to their meanness. *"Jah,* I like Jonathon, but not in that way."

"He's perfect for you." Lily giggled and poked Daisy in the ribs with her elbow.

Their father turned around to look at Jonathon, and then he glared at the twins. "It's been a long time since I had to scold the two of you, but if you can't behave, you'll spend the rest of the day in your rooms."

"Sorry, *Dat,"* Daisy said.

"Yeah, we didn't mean anything bad," Lily said, looking down at the table.

"I'm not sure what you meant, but you must watch your tongues. Small words can light great fires." He shook his head. "I'll be telling your *mudder* about this."

"Nee, Dat, please *nee,"* Lily pleaded.

"We'll go up to our rooms right now, but please don't tell *Mamm."* Daisy leaned over toward her father.

"She'll ask why you're in your rooms and I'll not lie," he said in a stern tone.

Lily nibbled a fingernail. "We won't do it again. We're sorry."

"See that you don't say anything like that again. And then we can forget the whole thing." His eyebrows pinched together as he shook his head. "I'll let it go this once if you watch your words."

"Denke, Dat." Lily glanced at Daisy with a look of relief. "We won't do it again. It was just a silly thing to say and we know that now."

"Just watch your tongues," he repeated.

Tulip did her best to hide her amusement at how

scared the twins were of their mother. Most people she knew were more scared of their fathers than their mothers, but their mother could be very stern sometimes and thought nothing of dishing out harsh punishment. Most of the punishments were in the order of staying in the house for two weeks and only being allowed to go to the meetings. That also meant having no friends over to visit.

The twins were quiet for the remainder of the wedding, which was most unlike them. Tulip couldn't stop glancing over at Nathanial. It was a nice feeling to potentially have someone special in her life. Even if nothing came of their date, it was nice to have that feeling of harmony and light within. Now she had a little taste of what it would be like to have a special man in her life just as Rose now had Mark.

CHAPTER 3

That night, when Nancy was at home with her husband, she sat on a chair in their bedroom and brushed out her long hair with slow, smooth strokes while a single tear trickled down her cheek. It wouldn't be the same without Rose in the house; it already felt empty.

"What's wrong?" Hezekiah asked.

"Nothing."

"Now come on; I know it's something. Are you sad about Rose moving out of the *haus?*"

"I'm happy she's married."

"That's not what I asked you."

"I'm just a little sad that our *kinner* have all grown up, and now our first *dochder* is married. I want them all to be young again. I want to turn back time, and have all of them small again and gathered around my feet pulling on my apron strings, annoying me. Now I'd give anything to have them surrounding me like that again." She wiped away tears from her eyes.

Hezekiah got up and stood behind his wife. Placing his

hands on her shoulders, he leaned over and kissed her on the cheek. "That's why we have to enjoy each and every moment. Each moment *Gott* gives us in this earthly home is precious."

"I wish I had enjoyed that time more when they were little. I kept looking forward to the time they'd be bigger, when I should've been enjoying them at the ages they were." She shook her head. "I had looked forward to the time when I could have an adult conversation with them and they would have their own opinions and ideas. Now that time has come, I miss their younger selves. You see, it is like they are each two different people—their younger selves and their older selves. I miss their younger selves. I know that doesn't make much sense and I'm babbling like a crazy woman."

"It makes perfect sense."

"People used to say to me, *Enjoy them while you can because they grow up so quickly.* I don't think I ever really did."

"There's no point in being upset about things that you cannot change, Nancy. Start now by enjoying each and every day for what joy it brings us."

"I suppose you're right." She inhaled deeply. "We can't turn back the clock."

"Now you can pass on your knowledge and your experience to our *kinner,* and to Shirley and soon to our other *grosskinner* when they arrive."

She laughed. "And they probably won't listen to me, just like I never listened to my parents."

Hezekiah chuckled. "You're probably right. We can only give them advice. It's up to them to follow it. Life's a journey, and we don't know in which direction the wind will blow our sails. All we can do is set our sails in the one we think is the right direction, with *Gott's* help, naturally."

Nancy breathed out heavily and then sighed. "I know I can't get the time back. I should enjoy the time I have with Tulip and the twins before they get married. And then when that happens it will feel very strange indeed. Do you realize that means the *haus* will be empty?"

"*Jah,* it'll be just like when we were newlyweds. We'll have the place to ourselves."

"I can look forward to that while also enjoying what's happening now."

"*Gut!* With the love you and I have for each other, our life together will be *wunderbaar.* I don't see that it could be any other way. We've been very blessed, you and I. We've always enjoyed each other's company and we'll go on doing that into our old age."

"I hope I go to *Gott* before you do," Nancy said while wondering why she was suddenly feeling so emotional. Normally, she wasn't a sensitive person prone to sudden pangs of nostalgia.

"There's no point talking about things like that. *Gott* takes us when he chooses."

"I know that, but what would I do without you?" She began to cry once again, and he encircled his arms about her.

"Whoever goes first, we won't be long without the other. We'll be together forever in *Gott's* Kingdom. This life is brief in comparison with eternity. And we'll spend eternity together. I think we can cope with maybe one or two years without the other, don't you?" He patted her on the shoulder and kissed her again.

"I know." She grabbed his hand and held it tight. "I know I'm being silly."

"*Nee*, you're not being silly. It's nice to hear how much you care for me. I haven't heard that in a while."

She turned to look him in the eyes. "You haven't?"

"I know how much you care for me, but it's nice to hear it every now and again."

"I'm sorry if I've been distracted. I've always done my best to be a good *fraa*."

"You've been the best *fraa* to me, and the best *mudder* to my *kinner*, that a man could have. And I don't know how you do half of the things that you do. You're truly an amazing woman."

She got up, stood in front of him, and wrapped her arms around him as he enfolded her in a hug. "I've truly been blessed. Rose has a perfect man and now it must be Tulip's turn."

"All in *Gott's* timing, Nancy, all in *Gott's* timing."

"That's exactly right." Nancy said with a little smirk turning the corners of her lips upward. Nancy closed her eyes and thought back to earlier that day. Rose's wedding had been beautiful. The ceremony had taken place outdoors between two overhanging trees. It was a beautiful sight to see how Rose looked adoringly into her husband's eyes.

She had seen that Jonathon's cousin, Wilhem, was sitting next to him and she noticed many girls looking at him while ignoring Jonathon. She thought it funny that girls placed such a high priority on the way men looked before getting to know them. Jonathon was a lovely man but because he was quiet and a little overweight, girls didn't give him a chance.

His handsome cousin won't be single for long, Nancy thought. Her worst nightmare would be that Tulip or any of her daughters would get married and go to live far away. She was certain that Tulip hadn't even noticed the handsome stranger who spent most of the wedding by his cousin, Jonathon's, side.

CHAPTER 4

Tulip managed to get out of the house on Saturday afternoon by telling her parents she was visiting friends. That wasn't a lie; Nathanial could be classed as a friend. She certainly didn't know him well enough to call him more than that. Because her mother was reprimanding the twins over something they'd forgotten to do, she just told Tulip she could go without asking any questions at all.

Tulip had taken the most reliable of their buggy horses and the smallest buggy. Once she found a spot near the café to park the buggy, she secured the horse and then smoothed down her dress with both hands. There was another horse and buggy on the same road and she wondered whether that might have been one that Nathanial had borrowed from the relatives he was staying with.

As soon as she turned the corner onto the main road, the café came into sight. She could see Nathanial's smiling face through the large window. He stood up and waved to her. Walking on the rough floorboards, she breathed in her favorite aroma—the smell of freshly-ground coffee.

"You look lovely, Tulip," he said as soon as she sat opposite him.

"*Denke.*"

He'd made her feel relaxed right away. She took in her surroundings. The café was large, with around twenty small tables inside and more tables outside under the awning on the broad sidewalk. On the mottled brown walls hung two large paintings that looked more like graffiti than art.

"I thought you wouldn't come."

Looking back at him, she gave a little giggle. "Why wouldn't I?"

"I thought your parents mightn't like me."

Tulip realized that he'd expected her to tell her parents where she was going. Somehow she'd gotten the opposite impression. She couldn't tell him that she hadn't told them because they might not approve of her seeing Jacob's brother —that might make him feel bad. "They don't know you."

"I met your *mudder* at the wedding. I haven't met your *vadder* yet, but I will since I'm staying longer. Now, what would you like to eat?"

"Just a coffee for me."

He pushed a menu over to her. "Nothing to eat?"

"*Nee, denke.* I've just eaten at home."

"I've just eaten too, but I can always eat more." He took the menu back and looked at it for a while before he said, "I'm going to have a steak sandwich. Can you help me eat it?"

"I could have a little."

"*Gut!*" He sprang to his feet to place their order at the register.

While he was gone, Tulip looked around, hoping that there was no one there who might happen to tell her parents she was sitting alone with a man. No, there was no one around that she knew. They were the only Amish couple in sight.

When he sat back down, she asked, "How is your *bruder?*"

"Jacob? He's okay. He's married now to Jessica. I'm not sure if you know that? And they've had a *boppli.*"

"That's nice. *Jah,* I did hear that." She had to change the embarrassing subject of Jacob and Jessica. "So, what kind of work are you looking for?"

"Anything. I learned the upholstery trade just like Jacob, but it's not something I want to do for the rest of my life. I like being out in the fresh air, and I like to build things."

"There should be plenty of that sort of work around."

"Which one?"

"Either, I suppose."

He chuckled. "I hope so. I'm starting my search on Monday. My *onkel* is asking around for me. He knows some builders. What is it that you like doing?"

"I don't have a job. I stay at home helping my *mudder.* There are only me and my two younger sisters at home now."

"Do you like doing that?"

She shuddered. "Not really. I'd rather be out of the

haus. I want to get some kind of a job, I just haven't worked out what I'd like to do."

"So, you want to get a job soon?"

"I do, if I could figure out what direction to go in. I like cooking, but that's all I can think of doing. Most jobs go to people with experience and I've heard it's hard to get a job without having worked somewhere else."

"You could work somewhere for free to gain experience."

"I suppose I could. I didn't think of that."

The waiter brought over their coffees.

"Thank you," Nathanial said, pushing the black coffee Tulip's way and keeping the latte in front of himself.

"The steak sandwich won't be long," the waiter said before he left.

Tulip picked up a spoon and then poured some sugar into her coffee. She normally didn't have sugar but the man sitting in front of her was making her lightheaded. Surely sugar would help steady her nerves.

They were halfway through their coffees when the steak sandwich arrived. It was huge and there was an extra plate containing a heaped helping of salad.

"Are you going to get through all that?"

He laughed. "I said I'd need help. I didn't realize it was going to be quite this large."

He cut a slice off his sandwich, placed it on the saucer that his coffee cup had stood on, and pushed it over to her. "You can start on that."

"I'll try, but I might not even be able to get through that amount."

He picked up his sandwich with both hands and bit

into it. Tulip picked up her portion and tried to eat in a ladylike manner, which was hard because butter was running onto her fingers and dripping onto the saucer.

Nathanial handed her a paper napkin and then used another one to wipe his hands.

"*Denke*. It's juicy."

He nodded because he still had a mouthful.

She ate a little, but that was enough. "I'm done. I can't possibly have any more."

He looked down at what was left of his sandwich. "Me too and we haven't even started on the salad."

"I'll just stick with my coffee."

"I hate wasting food," he commented.

"Maybe you can take it with you. They might put it into a container for you."

He shrugged. "Maybe. *Denke* for coming here today. I wanted to see you before your birthday."

She smiled at him, not knowing what to say. This was the first time she'd been alone with a man.

He picked up a napkin, leaned forward, and dabbed at her chin.

"What is it?" she asked.

"Just a little butter."

Now she felt embarrassed that she was smiling at him like a fool while she had melted butter on her chin. "*Denke*."

He scrunched up the napkin and put it on top of the salad.

"What does your *familye* think of you coming here for work?" she asked.

"They don't know yet. They think I'm visiting

Matthew. I don't see they'll mind when they find out. I'm from a big *familye* and most of us have gone in different directions. Jacob's still close to home, but I've got one *bruder* who moved to Canada to start a community there."

"That is a long way away."

"We might never see him again."

"That's sad."

"That's what he wanted. He married a girl from the community and then they decided that's what they wanted to do. No one was going to stand in their way."

"I'm glad both my brothers have stayed close by after they married, and I don't think Rose will go anywhere."

"Your *familye* sounds like they want to be close together."

"We do."

"Not all families are like that."

Tulip nodded and wondered what his family was like. Had he come to the wedding looking for a wife? Many of the young people went to weddings hoping to meet that special someone.

"Would you go on a buggy ride with me if I can borrow a buggy?"

"I'd like that." If that happened, she'd have to tell her mother who he was because he'd have to collect her from the house.

"*Gut!* I'll see what I can do. I might be able to take Matthew to the markets one day and then borrow his buggy. He works at the markets, you see."

"I know. Rose works at the markets too."

"I borrowed Matthew's buggy today. Hopefully, he'll let me borrow it again soon."

28

Tulip nodded, but wanted to know when he was thinking of taking her on this buggy ride. Buggy rides were the traditional way the Amish dated. She would've felt better if he mentioned a day or a time to lock it in rather than it being fuzzy and open-ended. Why were these things so hard? She should've gotten some tips from Rose before having coffee with him.

She drained the last of her coffee, which had gone cold. In her heart, she wondered whether Nathanial might have had a girl at home much like his brother had when he'd fooled Rose. Tulip didn't want to let Jacob's downfall influence her feelings toward Nathanial, and they wouldn't have if Nathanial had just made a time for their buggy ride. Now, things didn't quite feel right to her. She had to examine things with her head and not be carried away by feelings of the heart. That's what *Mamm* always said.

"All done?" he asked.

She nodded, hoping he'd suggest a romantic walk in the woods since it was such a lovely day.

"Gut! I'll walk you to your buggy."

Was that it? Was that all? Tulip was more than a little disappointed that there wouldn't be more to their afternoon together than sharing a steak sandwich.

She stood up, and they both walked out of the café.

"My buggy is around the corner," she said, still holding onto the hope he'd suggest they do something else.

They walked side-by-side in silence. Tulip hoped hard he'd suggest a time for that buggy ride and didn't want the conversation to go in a different direction. He, too, remained quiet.

When they reached her buggy, he said, "*Denke* for meeting me here. I'll see you again soon."

When Tulip was in the driver's seat, she looked over at him as he stood straight and tall. "You're coming to my birthday, aren't you?" She hoped that would prompt him to make a time.

"*Jah*, of course I am. I wouldn't miss it." He smiled at her and then moved forward and slapped her horse on the rump.

The horse moved onward and Tulip kept her eyes on the road ahead. Did he like her or what? Men sure were confusing creatures. Perhaps he had to find out if he could borrow the buggy again first before he made a time. While driving along the streets, she thought back over their conversation; she recalled he'd said he liked the outdoors. If that was so, then why hadn't he taken a table on the pavement in the fresh air? Was he worried that someone might see them together? Had he come here to her community and left a girlfriend at home just as his older brother had done before him?

Tulip did not want to end up in a bad situation. She'd think long and hard before going out with Nathanial again. Asking people about him might be the best idea. That way she could find out everything about him. Surely Matthew would know a lot since he was his cousin, or even Mark. Since Mark was recently married, she'd have to find out what she could about Nathanial from Matthew.

CHAPTER 5

Tulip woke up and stretched her arms over her head before she got out of bed. She smiled when she realized that today was her twentieth birthday. But that was before she remembered her mother had invited as many single young men as she possibly could to her birthday dinner that night. Now she groaned aloud. She hoped her mother wouldn't do to her what she'd done with Rose—try to match her with a man. Tulip was certain that Mark hadn't been her mother's first choice for Rose, but they were very happy.

"Happy birthday, birthday girl." The twins ran in and jumped on the edge of her bed.

"Argh! Just as well I'm awake."

"You're always awake at this time," Daisy said.

"What if I'd wanted to sleep in for my birthday?"

Lily giggled. "You have to get the eggs so you're not allowed to sleep in."

"How about one of you gets the eggs for me today?"

"*Nee!*" Lily scowled.

"I'll do it," Daisy said.

Lily suddenly changed her mind. "I'll come with you, Daisy."

The twins were gone like a whirlwind, as fast as they'd come into the room.

Tulip closed her eyes to enjoy another ten minutes sleep. Collecting the eggs was the first chore of the day and Tulip was only too happy when someone else did that for her.

She thought about the party and hoped her mother would make her a chocolate cake. No one could make a chocolate cake like her mother. The cakes her mother made were always so light and moist.

Unable to sleep, she pushed the blankets away from her and got out of bed. When she heard giggles, she walked over to the window and looked out. The twins were pushing and shoving each other as they walked toward the henhouse, tugging at the egg basket. It looked like they were arguing about who was to carry the basket. *I hope they don't do that when the basket is full of eggs.*

Tulip pulled on her bathrobe and popped her prayer *kapp* over her messy hair without even brushing it, and then headed downstairs. She'd have to tell her mother early that she wanted a chocolate cake because it had to be made with a special kind of cooking chocolate, and Tulip was certain they didn't have any more in the house —not with the twins around. The twins devoured any kind of chocolate as soon as it came through the door.

Tulip found her mother in the kitchen. "Morning, *Mamm.*"

Her mother looked over at her "Happy birthday, Tulip."

"*Denke, Mamm.*"

Her mother glared at her. "Why aren't you dressed?"

"I'm going to have a shower, and then I'll get dressed. I just wanted to ask if you could make a chocolate cake for me?"

"Chocolate cake for your birthday tonight?"

"*Jah.*"

"You had days to ask me that. Why leave it until now? I don't even have any ingredients for the chocolate cake."

"I could go to the store and get some for you."

She looked her up and down. "Not like that, you can't."

Tulip giggled. "I'm going to shower and then dress."

"Just make sure you don't let your husband see you like that of a morning."

Tulip frowned. "I'm not married."

"One day you will be."

"I'm sure he won't mind seeing me like this. What's wrong with how I look?" She looked down at her dressing gown. "It's just a bathrobe."

"You must always present yourself well."

Tulip knew her mother was annoyed with her for having to make a chocolate cake on short notice, and that's why she was picking on her. Her mother would've already had every minute of the day planned, right up until the time the guests arrived.

"I'll be the first one at the store and then I'll help you make the cake when I get back. What do you think about that?"

"It's your birthday! You can get the things from the store, but the twins will help me cook."

"Are you sure they even know how to cook?" Tulip giggled. All of them could cook, of course.

"We can cook better than anybody," Daisy said as she sailed through the back door with the egg basket over her arm.

"Better than you," Lily added.

"That's good. Then you can both help *Mamm* cook all day while I go to the store."

"I want to go too." Daisy pouted.

"Me too," Lily added.

"You both have to stay here and help *Mamm* cook."

"That's right. I would appreciate your help," their mother said.

"That's what we do every day. We do nothing else but help you cook and clean every single day."

Lily nodded at what Daisy said. "Yeah."

"You're not helping *me*," their mother said. "You both live here too; you're helping yourselves."

"And since it's my birthday, I choose to go to the store by myself," Tulip said before she raced up the stairs.

"I'm writing you out a list of things to get," her mother called after her.

CHAPTER 6

Tulip was glad to be allowed to go to the store by herself since the family only went to the store every fortnight. It was a rare thing for her to be allowed out in the buggy by herself. That's why she was so pleased her mother had let her go into town when she'd met with Nathanial. The family used to have only one horse and buggy, but thanks to a neighbor who had moved far away, they now had three buggy horses and two buggies. She caught the black horse in the paddock and slipped a rope around his neck and led him to the barn. They mostly used the bay gelding, but today she wanted to take the younger black one.

Her father wouldn't like her taking Damon, or 'Demon,' as her sisters called the horse. *Dat* considered the bay to be safer.

It was a half-hour journey each way. She considered the peace and quiet of this time alone a nice birthday present. It was a perfect time of year. Winter would soon be upon them, but today, the sun was shining.

As the horse and buggy clip-clopped toward the store in the lazy morning sun, she felt drowsy, as though she could easily go to sleep.

Rose had warned Tulip that their mother would soon try to find a man for her, but Tulip didn't think that was likely. Rose had been a dreamer and that's why their mother thought she needed help in finding a husband. Although it was a little troubling that *Mamm* had gone to such great lengths to invite so many people to her birthday party. Was this her mother's way of getting all the eligible young men in the community in one place?

As she drove along the streets in town, she decided to treat herself at one of the local cafés. While she was drinking coffee, she could look in the paper at the jobs section.

Rose still had her job helping the Walkers sell their flowers at the markets. She'd held that job for many years and it'd given her a good income. Having a job to go to every day would be far better than staying at home with her mother and the twins.

Now that Tulip was the oldest daughter at home, she felt the need to be independent, and with some extra money she'd be able to spread her wings and feel more grown up.

She stopped her buggy close to the supermarket and secured her horse. Damon had traveled well and hadn't stepped one hoof wrong. She patted him on his neck as a thank-you before she headed to the coffee shop, which was next to the supermarket. As soon as she walked in the door, she headed to a stand where the daily newspapers were held. Picking one up, she checked that it was today's paper. Once she saw it was, she carried it along as she headed to a table in the back of the room. Flipping the pages over, she found the job section.

"What can I get for you?"

She looked up to see a smiling young waitress. "I'll have a cup of coffee, thank you."

"Sure. Anything to eat today?"

"Last time I was here I had a cheesecake. Do you have any of those today?"

"We've got lemon cheesecake or chocolate."

"I'll have the lemon one, please." When the waitress was just about to walk away, Tulip said, "Excuse me?"

The waitress spun around. "Yes?"

"Do you know if you've got any jobs open here?"

"Not that I know of, but you could drop in a resume. That's how I got my job here."

Tulip nodded. "Thank you." A resume? She guessed that was a list of where she'd previously worked and a list of her skills. She didn't even have one and she had no idea how to put one together. The only experience she had was helping her mother cook and serve at functions.

When the waitress had gone, Tulip opened the paper once more and scanned the jobs on offer. There was nothing there for her. All the jobs required experience or some kind of qualifications.

TULIP HAD JUST TAKEN a large bite of her lemon cheesecake when she looked up to see an Amish man walk through the door of the café. She looked hard to see if it was someone she knew, but she'd never seen him before.

If he'd been one of the nearly three hundred guests at Rose's wedding, she certainly would've remembered. A man of his height and solid build would have made an impression.

He glanced in her direction and when their eyes met, he smiled at her and gave her a little nod. She gave the closest she could to a smile in return, as her mouth was still full of cheesecake. What bad timing!

When he turned back and grabbed a menu, she quickly swallowed and continued to study him. He'd removed his hat when he'd come inside, revealing unusual sandy-colored hair. Possibly it had started off light brown and the sun had streaked it with gold. It looked windswept and stopped above his shoulders. He was possibly one of the most handsome men she'd seen and he was definitely not from around the area.

After the waitress had said a few words to him, he took the menu with him and sat down at a table on the opposite side of the room. Now feeling awkward, she kept her head down, looking at the paper.

When the waitress approached him, Tulip listened to find out what he ordered, but she was too far away to hear anything. She looked in his direction. The waitress left, and the man turned his head in her direction. Tulip was quick to lower her gaze to the paper in front of her.

Tulip hurried to finish her coffee and the last mouthful of cheesecake. If she spent too much time away, her mother wouldn't have time to make her triple-layer chocolate cake.

She wiped her hands and mouth on the paper napkin and then hurried out of the coffee shop, careful not to look at the Amish man on the other side of the room. Tulip was only two steps out of the café when she heard someone calling.

"Miss! Miss!"

She turned around to see if the person was speaking to her. It was the waitress hurrying to catch up with her.

"Did I forget something?" Tulip asked.

"You forgot to pay."

Tulip covered her mouth with her hand. "I'm so sorry."

The girl offered a relieved smile.

"I'm not usually so forgetful." Her cheeks burning with embarrassment, Tulip walked back inside to pay. She daren't turn around to see if the man she'd been watching had noticed. "I normally go to places where I pay first," she explained to the woman as she handed over the money. When she'd paid, she hurried back outside.

Once she walked into the supermarket, she realized that she'd forgotten something else—the shopping list her mother had given her. She walked down each aisle trying to remember what was on that list. One thing Tulip recalled was the exact brand of cooking chocolate her mother liked to use. Now all they had to do was hide the chocolate from the twins until it was safely in the cake.

We have plenty of eggs and milk, also sugar, so what else could we possibly need? I know there's always lots of flour. She half filled her basket with things she thought her mother might need. As she tried again to remember what was on the list, she turned down the next aisle and nearly bumped into someone. She found herself face-to-face with the handsome Amish stranger who'd been in the coffee shop.

She stepped back. "I'm sorry."

He laughed and she walked around him.

"I saw you back there in the coffee shop."

She stared at him, not knowing what to say. All she could utter was, *"Jah?"*

"You nearly got away with it."

Tulip looked into his deep brown eyes that now crinkled at the corners. She thought about how the scene had unfolded when she'd forgotten to pay and she laughed.

"Maybe next time you should try running?"

"I'll have to remember that." She shook her head. "I'm still so embarrassed. I've never done anything forgetful like that before." Glancing down at the basket, she added, "Except forgetting my *mudder's* shopping list this morning, so that's two forgetful things on the same day."

"If that's the worst thing that happens today, it will have been a good day."

She smiled at him—her father would've said something similar to that. He seemed to have an easy-going and relaxed nature. He was also clean-shaven, so she knew he wasn't married. "Are you new around here, or are you passing through?"

"I'm just visiting. What about you?"

"I've lived here all my life." Her eyes dropped to the basket in her hands. "I should go. I've got people waiting for me."

She walked past him and he said nothing more. Once she was at the counter, she pulled all the goods out so they could be rung through the cash register. Tulip was certain she could feel the man looking at her. Turning around, she saw he was watching her with a smile on his face. She turned back around, now even more embarrassed.

If she were a braver person, she would've stopped and talked with him longer, but what would she say? The community was quite small, so soon enough she'd find out who he was and where he was staying. When she'd paid, she took her two bags of groceries and hurried out of the store.

Now she had two men to dream about—Jacob's younger brother, Nathanial, and this handsome stranger. Then a thought occurred to Tulip: she didn't even know his name.

CHAPTER 7

Once the birthday celebrations got underway that evening, Tulip quickly forgot the stranger she'd seen twice earlier that day.

Her two older brothers were there with their wives, and her baby niece, Shirley. Then the newlyweds, Rose and Mark, arrived.

Tulip was the first to scoop Shirley into her arms. She wasn't even a year old and she was quite heavy. She could say a few words, but that was all. Tulip tried to teach her to say, "Aunty Tulip"—all Shirley did was giggle.

Rose came up with her hands outstretched to take Shirley from her.

Once Rose had her niece in her arms, Tulip asked, "How's married life?"

"Everyone's asking me that."

"Well?"

"It's good. In fact, things are perfect."

"Perfect? Well, that's a big word." Tulip was used to

seeing Rose worrying about one thing after another. "You look satisfied and truly happy."

"I am. Now it's your turn to have *Mamm* trying to run your life."

Amy and Julie, their two sisters-in-law, joined their conversation.

"It never ends. First, everyone tells you that you should be married. When you get married, there's the pressure to have a child," said Amy.

Julie, Shirley's mother, continued, "Ah, but one's not good enough, because she'll need other children to play with. Meaning you have to produce another fast. And so it goes on. You have one child, then everyone's asking you when you'll have the second."

The girls giggled.

"I don't think we'll ever escape the pressure of other people's expectations. There always seems to be something else people think we should be doing," Tulip said.

Rose bounced Shirley on her hip. "My next project is to have one of these."

"Put your order in," Amy said, "but please don't have one before me because I got married first."

"I can't promise," Rose said with a grin.

Tulip was distracted by people coming through the front door.

"How many people are coming, Tulip?" Amy asked.

"I think *Mamm* invited the whole community and then some. Excuse me, I'll have to greet everyone."

The guests were served buffet-style in the kitchen. Everyone picked up a plate and, at her mother's direction, walked clockwise around the table serving themselves from the bowls in the center. Tulip's mother looked on, redirecting anyone who dared walk counterclockwise.

Taking center stage on the table was a large triple-layer chocolate cake. Tulip was upset that Nathanial hadn't come. Surely if he liked her enough to ask her on a buggy ride, he should've come to her birthday party. Especially after saying he would be there. Tulip hoped he was only late, held up by something, and he'd still arrive.

LATER THAT EVENING, Rose and Tulip were talking again.

"I want to get a job like you've got, Rose."

"What would you do?"

"I don't know exactly. I can cook and clean and I suppose I can sell things like you do. I've helped at the flower stall often enough."

"What about Audrey Fuller's cake shop? She's expanding it. She'll need more staff."

"Is she really?"

Rose nodded.

"That's a good idea. I'll get in before she starts advertising for people."

"Yeah, do it. I think you'd like working there." Rose looked around the room and then she fixed her eyes in one spot.

"What is it, Rose?" Tulip turned her head to see what Rose was staring at.

"Look at *Mamm* over there. It looks like she's interviewing for a new husband for you."

Tulip shook her head. "You're lucky you found Mark when you did."

"I didn't need to find him; he was there all the time."

Tulip sighed. "I've got nobody who's been there all the time like that. What am I going to do about *Mamm?*"

"If you get a job, she mightn't be so focused on you."

"I hope so, and then she can start on the twins," Tulip said.

"Yeah, they're nearly old enough to marry now."

The two sisters giggled.

CHAPTER 8

The next day, Tulip put Nathanial out of her mind and wasted no time in setting about looking for a job. She'd already done most of her morning chores when she walked into the kitchen to ask her mother for permission to be gone for a good part of the day.

"*Mamm,* can I take the buggy to go into town today?"

Her mother turned around from the stove where she was cooking breakfast.

"What for? You went into town yesterday."

"Rose told me that Audrey Fuller might be looking for someone to work in her cake store."

The twins giggled, and Daisy said, "Haven't you had enough cake? You ate your birthday cake nearly by yourself yesterday."

"Yep, and no one else could get any," Lily added.

"I only had two pieces and they were small ones." Tulip looked back at her mother as she sat down at the kitchen table. "Rose said Audrey's expanding her store, and I want to get in first before she thinks about putting an ad in for someone."

"That sounds like a good idea, but I didn't even know you wanted a job." Her mother placed a plate of eggs in front of her.

"I do. I've been thinking about it for some time."

"Well, you better get into town and see her."

"Denke, Mamm."

"Now, eat your breakfast."

"If you can fit it in after all that cake you ate last night. It's a wonder you're not twice the size."

"Hush, Daisy," their mother said.

"You don't have to work, Tulip," Lily said.

Tulip had a mouthful of eggs, and when she swallowed, she answered, "I know that, Lily, but I want to."

"Could we go into town too, *Mamm?*" Daisy asked. "While she goes to the cake shop we can do something else by ourselves."

Tulip frowned, hoping her mother wouldn't let them. She didn't want them around distracting her or saying silly things when she was trying to get a job.

Thankfully, her mother read her anxious expression.

"Nee. It's best if you stay here. We've got a big clean-up day ahead of us."

The twins' mouths dropped open, and Daisy said, "That's not fair! Tulip should help; it was her party."

Tulip ate her breakfast in silence, feeling relieved that she was escaping the clean up.

~

TULIP WALKED into the cake shop to see that the space had already been extended. When she'd been there last, there was no room for anyone to sit down. Now there were tables inside, and more outside on the pavement. She stepped past the tables to speak to the young girl behind the counter.

"Is Mrs. Fuller in today?"

"Yeah, she's out in the back."

"Could I speak with her?"

"I'll get her."

The girl she'd been speaking to wasn't Amish, but she knew a couple of the girls who worked for Audrey were Amish.

When Audrey came into the front of the store, she looked pleased to see her. "Tulip! Happy birthday for yesterday. I heard you had a big birthday dinner at your place last night."

"*Denke.* I did." Tulip gave a little giggle.

"What can I do for you?"

"I was hoping you might be looking for an extra person to work here?"

Audrey narrowed her eyes as she scrutinized her. "I am looking for one more person. Have you had any experience?"

Tulip's shoulders drooped. "Not really. I've only worked for my *mudder* at weddings and things like that."

"That might count for experience. Your mother is a very good manager. I could give you a trial for three weeks and see how we work together. I start all my girls on trials. I'd have to show you how to work the register and how to make coffee barista-style."

"Really?"

"Jah."

"I'd love to learn how to do everything. *Denke* so much."

"Are you looking for full time or part time work?" Audrey asked.

"Full time, but I can do whatever you'd like."

"I'm looking for someone full time. It wouldn't be until the first of next month. Would you be able to start then?"

"I certainly would. *Denke* again, Mrs. Fuller."

She chuckled. "The girls here all call me Audrey when we're in the shop."

"Okay."

CHAPTER 9

*T*ulip had been working at the cake shop for the past three months. She'd done well right from the start, and Audrey had quickly offered her a permanent position. She got along fine with the other staff. Stacey, the girl she'd met that first day, was the only *Englischer,* and the rest of the girls were Amish. Melinda, a girl in her mid-twenties, was the manager whenever Audrey was absent. Audrey started work early and generally left at eleven in the morning.

Tulip was wiping down the counter in the back room, and when she heard the girls giggling, she looked into the store and saw Jonathon Byler buying a cupcake. When Tulip went out front, she noticed that Jonathon was now outside by himself, drinking a cup of coffee with his cupcake on a plate on the table.

"Look at him, sitting out there by himself. That's why he's so fat! He eats cake every day. He looks ridiculous," one of the girls said while another one giggled.

"Back to work," Melinda said, trying to break things up.

"Why aren't you laughing, Tulip?" Stacey asked.

"I don't think it's funny to be like that with people."

"Tulip's in love with Jonathon," Stacey said.

"I'm not in love with him. I just know that he's nice, and it's mean to laugh at him." She glanced at him and hoped he didn't hear their laughs. "I'm going to wipe down the tables outside." After she had picked up a cloth, she headed outside.

"Hello, Jonathon," Tulip said as she wiped down the table next to his.

Jonathon glanced up at her. "Hello, Tulip. I didn't know you were working here. How are you today?"

"Fine! Is there anything else you'd like?"

"*Nee, denke.* My cousin's joining me today. You could join us if you'd like. Do you get a break or anything?"

"I'm actually due for a half hour break." She glanced at the girls inside who were smiling at the pair of them talking. "I'll get myself a cup of coffee and something to eat and I'll come back out."

"Okay, *gut.*"

Tulip hurried inside and asked Melinda if she could take her break right now.

After Melinda agreed, one of the girls said, "You *are* in love with him; you're having coffee with him."

"So what?" Once she had paid for her coffee and a raisin bun, she made herself a coffee, placed a bun on a plate, and hurried outside with them to join Jonathon. She hated anyone to be made fun of.

"Which cousin are you waiting for?" Tulip asked.

"I don't know if you've met him. He comes here every now and again when my *vadder* has work for him." He looked over her shoulder. "Here he is now."

Tulip glanced behind her. It was the same man she'd seen a few months ago, around the time of her birthday. She looked back to the front and he sat down with them.

Jonathon introduced the pair of them. The handsome man's name was Wilhem Byler.

"Actually, we've met before, but I didn't get your name last time."

Tulip giggled. "I remember."

His eyes dropped down to her food. "I hope you've paid for that?"

She laughed. "Your memory is too good. I paid for it and I work here." She told Jonathon about forgetting to pay and leaving the café and the waitress having to come running after her. Then the three of them laughed.

"Actually," Wilhem began, "I was at your *schewschder's* wedding a while back. That's when I first saw you."

"At Rose's wedding?"

He nodded.

"I didn't see you there."

One side of Wilhem's mouth twisted into a crooked smile. "I saw you."

Tulip was pleased about him saying that. He was almost flirting with her and his voice lowered when he spoke. "How often do you come here?" she asked.

"Every now and again when my *Onkel* Phillip has construction work for me."

"That's my *Dat*," Jonathon said.

Tulip nodded at Jonathon. Of course she knew

Jonathon's father. She looked back at Wilhem. "Ah, so you do construction work—building work?"

"*Jah.* There are a few builders I work with back home, and now my *onkel* is going to be needing me from time to time. I'm happy to help out here."

Tulip smiled at the thought of him visiting their community more. Through the large glass window, Tulip looked to see that the girls weren't laughing anymore—not with the handsome man now sitting at the table with them.

Tulip was so nervous sitting next to him that she barely heard any more of the conversation. She hoped she was responding with the right words in the right places.

When Jonathon's cousin said goodbye and left, Tulip suddenly realized her break time had nearly run out. "I'll have to get back to work, Jonathon. *Denke* for inviting me."

"I'll see you soon. *Denke* for sitting with us."

Tulip stood and gathered the empty cups.

"Wait, Tulip!" Jonathon said.

"What is it?"

"Do you think you could put a good word in for me with Chelsea?"

Chelsea was one of the young Amish girls she worked with. "You like her?"

He nodded.

"Okay, I'll do it. But not right away, or it will seem phony. I'll wait for the right time."

"*Denke,* Tulip. I'll leave it in your hands."

Tulip walked back into the store with the plates and cups they'd used.

"You were a while," Chelsea said.

Glancing up at the clock, Tulip said, "I only had my half hour."

"Did you have fun with your new boyfriend?" Stacey asked.

Tulip spun around. "He's very nice."

"Who is? Jonathon, or that man who sat down with you? That was the real reason you sat out there with Jonathon, wasn't it?" Stacey asked. "He didn't stay very long."

"He's Jonathon's cousin." Tulip ignored the rest of the comment.

When Stacey said something else about Jonathon, Melinda cut across her, "Back to work now, and no more talk about the customers."

The girls stopped talking.

Later in the day, Stacey whispered to Tulip, "No need to get upset. Maybe you really are in love with Jonathon."

To Tulip, all the teasing and gossiping was just like being at home with the twins.

CHAPTER 10

$\mathcal{N}$athanial had never gotten back to her about the buggy ride he'd mentioned. Now that she'd met Jonathon's handsome cousin, Wilhem, she was dreaming about him instead.

The next time Tulip saw Nathanial again was at Lucy and Peter Bontrager's wedding. There were many visitors from out of town at the wedding, which was held at Lucy's parents' house, in their yard. As always, Tulip's mother was at the forefront of organizing the food, along with the bride's mother.

"Do you know who's here, Tulip?" her mother asked her.

"Who?"

"Jacob Schumacher's *bruder*. His name is Nathanial."

Tulip was pleased he was there. Maybe they would go on that buggy ride soon. She hadn't seen Wilhem again and didn't know if he'd ever be back. "Okay. I haven't seen him about."

"I think he was one of the boys you were talking with at Rose's wedding."

Tulip shrugged her shoulders. "Not sure. It was a long time ago."

"Stay away from him, if you happen to see him."

"Why, *Mamm?*"

Her mother's mouth fell open. "You know what happened when Jacob visited the community, don't you?"

"*Jah,* but his *bruder* can't be held responsible for Jacob's actions. Anyway, Jacob did the right thing and married that girl, so that's at least a *gut* thing." She had to make her mother think that he was okay, otherwise she'd never be able to go anywhere with him.

"Shh! Someone might hear." Her mother shook her head. "They are branches of the same tree. There are such things as bad seeds. I'm just warning you that if he's anything like Jacob, he'll be looking for prey. And by prey, I mean young girls who don't know any better."

"*Jah, Mamm.*"

"I mean it, Tulip. I have the benefit of many more years' experience than you do. You'd do well to listen to me."

"I do. I listen to you all the time."

"*Gut!* Now help Rosemary take those dishes out." Her mother pointed to the large collection of plates that had to be carried out and placed on each table.

Tulip did as she was asked. As she walked amongst the crowd, she looked around for Nathanial. Just as she placed half a dozen dinner plates on one of the tables, she caught a glimpse of him, and he caught her eye and smiled. She quickly looked away in case her mother was

AMISH TULIP

watching, and then she hurried back for more plates. Tulip believed there was no such thing as 'bad seeds.' Her mother was simply being over-protective.

When her mother allowed Tulip time to eat later that day, she hurried to one of the tables at the back of the yard, hoping there would be food left in the bowls in the center of that table. There was. She picked up an empty plate and spooned food onto it before she sat down.

"Did you cook the food?"

She looked up to see it was Nathanial who'd just walked up to her. He sat down next to her as she finished her mouthful. If only she knew why he'd never gotten back to her about going on the buggy ride. That really bothered her. Did that mean he wasn't interested in her after all?

"*Nee.* I just had the job of running the plates in and out. I'm on a break, and soon I'll have to take the plates back to the kitchen."

He put out his hand as though he was meeting her for the first time. "I'm Nathanial Schumacher."

She kept the charade going. "Hello, I'm Tulip Yoder."

His gaze dropped to her food and he tipped his head. "Go ahead. Don't let me stop you from eating."

"Have you moved here or are you visiting?" she asked to carry on with the act of having just met him.

"I'm doing some visiting around different places to see where I'd like to settle down."

Tulip finished what was in her mouth. "Where are you from?"

"Oakes County."

"Are you Jacob's *bruder?*"

59

"*Jah*, but don't hold that against me." He laughed.

"I met him. He visited here a while back to work for your *Onkel* Harry."

"Before your new *bruder*-in-law, Mark, stole his job."

Tulip narrowed her eyes at him. That's not how she remembered things at all.

"I'm joking. I'll have to brush up on my funny skills —humor."

She smiled. "It's not that. I was just trying to remember what happened. Jacob wasn't here long before he went back home and since then Mark's been working with your mutual *onkel* making buggies."

"That's correct."

When he smiled, Tulip saw kindness in his eyes. Her mother had to be wrong about him. Although she wasn't sure if she'd forgiven him about forgetting their buggy ride.

"And now you know all about me, Tulip, tell me something about yourself."

"There's not much to tell. I started working in a bakery a few months ago and that's what I do every day."

"Your *familye?*"

She pointed to her father who was talking with the bishop. "That's my *vadder*, and my mother is in the kitchen, unless she's spying on me right now to see who I'm speaking with. I've got three sisters around somewhere and two older brothers."

"Your *vadder's* a deacon?"

"*Jah.*"

"That must be hard."

"*Nee*, not really."

"I have a friend whose *vadder* is the bishop and she finds it awkward. She says that everyone thinks she should be perfect."

"It's a little like that sometimes."

"Where is the bakery?"

"Just off Church Street, in Baker's Lane."

"I might have to try some samples."

Tulip smiled as she ate another spoonful of food. Maybe he did have some unreliable traits, as his brother had.

"We never went on that buggy ride," he said.

"Buggy ride?" She wouldn't let on that she remembered anything about that.

"*Jah*, you promised you'd go on one with me."

"Did I?"

"*Jah*, you did." He laughed. "I'm not going to let you back out of it. How about we go on one this week?"

"What day were you thinking?"

"How about Wednesday night? I'll take you home after the softball game."

"Okay."

CHAPTER 11

*L*ater that day, Tulip regretted agreeing to the buggy ride with Nathanial when she saw Wilhem Byler again. Her hands were full of dishes and she was walking to the kitchen with Rose.

"Tulip."

She stopped to talk with him and Rose kept walking. "Hello, Wilhem. I didn't expect to see you here."

"Lucy's one of my cousins."

Tulip laughed. "Lucy is a cousin of yours, and Jonathon is too?"

"Yeah, Lucy is a cousin on my *mudder's* side and Jonathon is a cousin on my *vadder's* side."

"Everyone has so many cousins I can't keep track."

"I was hoping to see you here." He looked down at the plates. "Can I carry those for you?"

She shook her head. "I'll take these to the kitchen and come back out. Stay right there." Tulip scurried to the kitchen, dumped the dirty dishes with all the others beside the sink, wiped her hands on a dishtowel, and hurried outside to see Wilhem.

"Has your *onkel* got some work for you? Is that why you're back?" she asked.

"*Jah,* I'll be here for about six weeks." He looked around. "Shall we take a walk and get away from the crowd?"

She whipped her head around, looking for her mother, and when she couldn't see her anywhere, she said, "Okay."

Together they walked behind the food tables and out to a fence that separated two fields from the yard.

"Ah, silence," Tulip said.

"It's nice, isn't it?"

"It sure is."

"Tulip, I've been looking for you. I'm hoping I can see a bit more of you while I'm here."

"I'd like that."

"I've heard there's a softball game on one night soon. I normally wouldn't go, but if you're going I'd go there."

She had to think fast. Tulip couldn't let Wilhem see her with Nathanial. They both seemed nice, but she was now confused and didn't know which one she liked better. First there was no one and now she had two young men she liked. "I don't like softball." That was the truth.

"Okay. How about we go out somewhere else? Just the two of us?"

She nodded. "That sounds *gut.*"

"What if I collect you one day after you finish work?"

"Okay."

"We could go out for dinner somewhere nice."

"I'd like that."

It was when he smiled she knew she preferred Wilhem to Nathanial. And her mother would be pleased about her choice too, since *Mamm* still hadn't gotten over how Nathanial's brother had upset Rose.

"Monday, then?"

"Monday would be perfect." She glanced through the trees at the women collecting everything from the tables. "I'd better go back and help, or I'll face my *mudder's* wrath."

"I'll look forward to Monday," he called after her.

She hurried away, wondering how she could get herself out of this mess. She'd agreed to see Wilhem on Monday for dinner, and then on Wednesday she was going on a buggy ride with Nathanial. It wasn't right. She should've just chosen one or the other, but she hadn't expected Wilhem to suddenly turn up out of the blue like he had. To make matters worse, who would she tell her parents was driving her home from the softball game?

The best thing she could do, she decided, was tell Nathanial she couldn't make it on Wednesday.

After she took another load of dishes to the kitchen, she looked around for Nathanial. She couldn't see him, but found Matthew, the cousin he was staying with.

"Matthew, where's Nathanial?"

"Hi, Tulip. He's left already."

"Gone home? Back to Oakes County?"

"Back to our *haus,* not back to *his* home."

"I see."

"Do you want me to give him a message? I'm heading there now myself."

"*Nee.* It was nothing. *Denke,* Matthew."

. . .

THE REST OF THE DAY, Tulip was worried about the mess she'd created. She couldn't talk anything over with her younger sisters because they'd only spill the beans to their mother, who'd have an absolute fit if she learned she'd arranged to go out with Nathanial Schumacher.

Maybe Nathanial won't even go to the softball game. He forgot all about our buggy ride once before.

Tulip decided to do nothing and let things run their natural course.

~

THE NEXT DAY WAS SUNDAY. There was no meeting that day as they held their meetings fortnightly and had just met the previous Sunday.

As she was wondering what to do for the day, she remembered her words to Jonathon. She'd agreed to put a good word in for him with Chelsea. Work was sometimes hectic, and besides that, it wasn't a good place to talk about personal things. If the other girls heard them discussing Jonathon, they'd laugh about him and that wouldn't help Jonathon get closer to Chelsea.

Later that day, Tulip knocked on the door of Chelsea's home.

Chelsea's mother opened the door. "Hello, Tulip. Come in. Are you here to see Chelsea?"

"*Jah,* is she home?"

"Chelsea!" her mother hollered.

Chelsea came running down the stairs and stopped abruptly at the bottom. "Hello, Tulip."

"Hi, I was going for a long walk and saw your *haus* and thought I'd stop by and say hi."

"You walked all the way from your *haus?*"

"I'll get you girls some lemonade."

"Nee, we can get it, *Mamm,"* Chelsea said.

The two girls sat at the kitchen table. "So, tell me what's going on. What's the real reason you're here?" Chelsea's brown eyes bored through hers.

Tulip giggled. "I love to walk, to go on really long walks. And I saw your *haus.*"

"Come on, Tulip. We've lived next to each other for a really long time and you've never come here and I've never gone to visit you. What is it?"

Tulip sipped on her lemonade. She couldn't betray a confidence.

"Is it about work? Is that it? Am I getting the sack—fired—cut loose?" She clutched at her throat.

"Nee, nothing like that. Anyway, no one would tell me anything like that. I was the last to start so I'd be the first to go."

"What is it, then?"

"Can't a girl talk to another girl?" Tulip asked.

"Jah, of course."

"You see, since Rose left and married Mark, I feel a little … a little lonely."

"You need a friend?"

"Kind of. I mean, there's the twins, but …"

"Yeah, well, I know what *they're* like. They're all giggles

67

all the time. I don't know how you live under the same roof as them."

"Me either!"

"Between you and me, I find them annoying," Chelsea said. "Oh, I shouldn't have said that. That was mean."

"See? We're quite alike," Tulip commented.

Chelsea smiled. "I suppose we are. I guess a girl can never have too many friends."

"Exactly."

"Cheers to that," Chelsea said, offering her glass to connect with Tulip's.

Tulip 'clinked' glasses with her, and the girls giggled. Now, how would she raise the subject of Jonathon without Chelsea knowing that was the real reason she was there? There was no way she could. The subject of Jonathon would have to wait for another day.

What she'd said was right, anyway. She really could use a friend now, since Rose had married. There was a gap in her life that Chelsea might be able to fill. Chelsea wasn't one of the girls at work who had been making fun of Jonathon. She'd remained quiet. That was a hopeful sign for Jonathon.

"I'm glad you came here, Tulip. I've always wanted to be friends with you, but you've always been surrounded by your sisters."

"I'm glad too."

"Do you want to see my room?"

Tulip nodded and together the girls left their half-full lemonade glasses on the kitchen table and climbed the stairs of the farmhouse.

. . .

Tulip told Chelsea about Wilhem collecting her from work on Monday and then taking her out for dinner.

Her friend told her that she'd officially met him at the Bontrager wedding.

She didn't tell Chelsea that she'd also agreed to be taken home from the softball game by Nathanial. She was still trying to figure out what to do about that.

CHAPTER 12

*I*t was the middle of the day when Jonathon made his daily trip to the cake store.

"It's Jonathon."

"Why don't you serve him, Chelsea?" Tulip suggested.

"Okay. Don't you want to? Isn't he a friend of yours?"

Tulip nodded. "He is, but he'd rather you serve him."

Chelsea frowned at her but when Tulip disappeared into the back room, Chelsea had no choice but to serve Jonathon when he walked in.

Tulip looked at the other two girls talking as they worked in the backroom. It was nearly into their busy time of day and soon the store would be flooded with people. For now, Tulip was pleased they hadn't noticed Jonathon so they wouldn't say mean things.

When Tulip peeped out and saw Jonathon was now sitting at one of the tables on the pavement, she joined Chelsea behind the counter.

"Does he want a cup of coffee? I'll make him one if he does," Tulip said.

"You like him, don't you, Tulip?"

"Yes, of course I do."

"But not as a boyfriend?"

"*Nee,* just as a friend," Tulip said.

Chelsea asked, "Why not as a boyfriend?"

Tulip looked up at the ceiling while trying to examine why she didn't like him as a boyfriend.

"Is it because he's quiet and doesn't talk to many people or is it because he's fat?"

Tulip knew Chelsea wasn't being mean.

"I don't think it's either of those. There just isn't that spark I feel when I like a boy."

"Not like the spark you have with Wilhem?"

"I suppose that's true."

"I'm glad you don't say rude things about him like the other girls," Chelsea whispered.

"Everyone's different. They should put themselves in Jonathon's shoes and see how they'd feel about the sniggers. I reckon he can feel it even if he can't hear them. He's a good and kind person."

"That's true," Chelsea said.

Tulip was pleased she'd been able to do what Jonathon had asked. She didn't know if Chelsea would ever feel the way Jonathon wanted her to feel, but at least she was doing her best without being overly obvious. At least, that's what she hoped.

"Are you nervous about tonight?" Chelsea whispered to Tulip just before closing time.

"I am, but I'm trying not to be nervous."

"It's very romantic."

"Is it?"

"*Jah,* a handsome stranger comes to the community and you're the only girl he's interested in."

Tulip giggled. "I didn't think of it like that."

When closing time came, Tulip waited outside the store, nervous about the situation she'd gotten herself into. She still hadn't canceled Wednesday night with Nathanial. She decided she had to put the situation about Wednesday night totally out of her mind for now in order to enjoy her time with Wilhem.

Her heart pounded in her chest when she saw Wilhem in the buggy heading toward her.

"It's nice to see you again," he said when she climbed in and sat next to him.

Looking into his soft brown eyes, she said, "And you."

He smiled and then gave the horse an order to move forward.

"Where are we going?" Tulip asked.

"I've made reservations at a place just outside town. It's an old Amish farmhouse that has been converted into a restaurant."

"I think I know the one. I've never been there but I've heard it's good."

THE WAITER PLACED their napkins on their laps, which Tulip thought an odd thing to do, but perhaps that's what they did in posh restaurants. She was only used to diners and coffee shops. The waiter then handed them menus before he disappeared. Soon after, another waiter came to take their drink order.

"Should we get a bottle of wine?" Wilhem asked studying the list in his hands.

"I don't drink alcohol," Tulip said.

He closed the drinks menu, leaned over, and said, "Neither do I."

Tulip was pleased that they had another thing in common. "Iced tea sounds good to me."

Once they'd made their orders and were alone, Wilhem leaned forward slightly. "Tulip, why is a girl like you still single?"

"I can't marry just anyone. I've been waiting for the right person."

"That's a good answer."

"Everyone thinks a girl should be married before she is twenty, but not everyone has to follow the usual pattern of things. I wouldn't mind if I never got married."

"Don't you want *kinner?*"

"I suppose that would be nice someday, but it's not the end of the world if I don't have any." Now she knew she'd let her mouth run away with her when she saw that Wilhem looked puzzled. She did her best to rectify the situation. "I guess I want what every girl wants, but if it doesn't happen ..." She stopped abruptly. Perhaps she was digging herself a deeper hole. Here was a potential husband sitting right in front of her, a man who obviously interested in her, and she was telling him she didn't care whether she got married or not. She looked into his eyes, wondering how to get herself out of the mess.

He gave a laugh. "You're quite different, compared with other girls I've met."

"And you've met a lot of girls on your travels?" she asked, trying to change the subject.

"Not really. I only go from home to here. They're the only places that I've been. Most girls think about nothing else other than being married, and that's all they talk about, and hint at."

Tulip tried to assess how the early part of the date was going. It was possibly a good thing that she was different from the other girls. She wondered exactly how many girls he'd been out with. A man as handsome as Wilhem could've been on many dates.

When they were halfway into their main course, he began to talk about what he wanted in life, and then added, "I'm thinking of moving here."

"You are?"

"I've been talking about it with Jonathon. He wants to move out of his parents' house and we figured we would share a *haus.*"

Tulip's immediate thoughts were about Chelsea. She knew Chelsea might be more interested in Jonathon if he were living away from his parents' home; it would make him seem more of a man and more independent.

"So what do you think of that idea?" he asked.

"I think it's a great idea. Would you get enough work here?"

"I would. Besides my *onkel,* there are other people I've met that said they could give me work."

Tulip licked her lips. That was the best news she'd heard for a long time.

"And when do you think this will happen?"

"Within the next few months. Jonathon is already looking for a *haus* and as soon as he finds one, I can put my plan into motion."

"So you've moved on from thinking about it. You're actually going to do it?"

He nodded. *"Jah.* I guess I should've said that. I hope you're pleased."

"Won't your parents miss you?"

"I won't be that far away and I can always visit them."

At the end of their meal, Wilhem looked across at her. "Can I see you again soon, Tulip?"

"I'd like that. Can we talk about that on Sunday after the meeting?"

He drew his eyebrows together. "Okay."

She hoped he wouldn't ask why and was glad when he didn't.

CHAPTER 13

On Wednesday, Tulip had every intention of not going to the softball game. If she wasn't there, then Nathanial wouldn't be able to drive her home. As she was eating dinner on Wednesday night, her father asked her to drive the twins to the game. The twins were old enough to drive the buggy, but their father had never allowed them to do so after a particularly nasty incident where they galloped a horse too hard against their father's instructions.

Tulip had no choice but to agree to take the twins. And it was too far to drop them off and then collect them when it finished, so she would have to stay through the whole thing. She only hoped that Nathanial would forget about their former arrangement. A smile twitched at the corners of her lips when she realized that she wouldn't be able to go on a buggy ride with him if she had to take the twins home. It was the perfect way out.

. . .

As soon as Tulip stopped the buggy at the field where the baseball game was being held, the twins jumped out and ran off to meet their friends, giggling all the way.

Tulip secured the horse and then looked into the crowd to find Nathanial.

She took a deep breath and walked toward the group of people. She saw him sitting by himself and then made her way to him.

"There you are," he said, looking up at her. "Sit with me."

She sat down. "I'm afraid I won't be able to go on a buggy ride tonight after all."

"That's disappointing. I was looking forward to it. I even borrowed the nicest buggy and best horse I could."

"I'm sorry. I have to drive my sisters home. *Dat* doesn't trust them to drive the buggy."

"That's no problem. I could follow you home and then we could go from there."

Tulip hadn't thought of that. "The thing is that—"

"You haven't told your folks we were planning on going on a buggy ride?"

She looked down at the dirt underneath her black lace-up boots. *"Nee,* I haven't."

"I see. They wouldn't like me taking you home because I'm Jacob's *bruder?"*

She shook her head, not wanting him to think her parents would judge him by what his brother had done. Her mother did, but her father probably wouldn't if he knew about Nathanial and him asking her out.

"That's all right; you don't need to say anything further."

She frowned. "You've got it all wrong. It's nothing like that."

"It looks like I'll have to prove myself to them. I'll introduce myself to your *vadder* at the Sunday meeting."

"What will you say?" Tulip hadn't figured on that.

"I'll just say, *Hi, I'm Jacob's brother, Nathanial.*" He laughed. "Don't look so worried."

"It's always a worry. You don't know what my parents are like."

"From the look on your face, I've got a pretty good idea."

Tulip laughed. It seemed he was making an effort to impress her family so that meant that he was taking her seriously. But where did that leave Wilhem? She'd gotten herself into a right mess. She liked Nathanial but she preferred Wilhem and what's more, Wilhem was moving to the community and she had no idea what Nathanial's plans were.

"I was really looking forward to our buggy ride," he said.

She remembered back to months ago when he'd first mentioned going on a buggy ride, and hadn't followed through.

He continued, "Like I said, I'll get your *vadder* on my side and then everything will be a whole lot easier."

"I don't know about that. There's still my *mudder.*" Tulip wished she'd kept quiet. If he talked to her mother, he might get an earful. Then, both her mother and father would think there was something happening between her and Nathanial.

When the game was underway, she looked over at the

79

opposite side to a group of seats. There she saw Jonathon talking with Chelsea. They were sitting side-by-side and looking like they were good friends. Tulip smiled and hoped that she'd been instrumental in them speaking with one another like that.

Chelsea hadn't mentioned she was going to the softball game, but then neither had Tulip mentioned her plans to stay home, until she'd been asked to drive for her sisters. It wouldn't be a good idea for Chelsea to see her with Nathanial, as Chelsea knew about her dinner date with Wilhem.

"Who are you looking at?" Nathanial's eyes had followed her gaze.

"Just my friend over there. Her name is Chelsea. I work with her at the bakery."

"Is that her talking to that large man?"

"*Jah*. His name is Jonathan and he's also a good friend of mine."

"Tulip, are you sure that there isn't something standing in between us?"

"What do you mean? Like what?"

"Like what happened when my *bruder* was here in this community? And what he did before I got here? I wouldn't like to be judged by my *bruder*. I'm nothing like him and never have been. You're not that type of girl, are you?"

"What type of girl do you mean?"

"A judgmental kind of girl who won't give a man a chance."

"*Nee*, of course not. It's nothing like that. You've got everything all wrong. It's not about you. It's just that *Dat* recently got a new horse and buggy so us girls could use it, but he still doesn't trust the twins completely after what happened."

He crossed one leg over the other. "Why, what happened? Why doesn't he trust the twins?"

"A neighbor moved away and gave us their buggies and horses. One of the twins galloped one of the poor horses too hard and he was in a lather of sweat when he got home. It'll be a long time before she can drive the buggy again. I've never seen my *vadder* lose his temper, but that day he was close to it. I can tell you that much."

Nathanial laughed.

"It wasn't funny. You should've been there to see it."

"I'm sorry. I shouldn't laugh. Isn't that what horses are meant to do? It won't hurt the horse to have a good run."

"It wasn't that so much. It was because the horse was too young, or something, to race so hard like that. Anyway, *Dat* had already told them to take it easy with the horse and only walk him."

"Is your *vadder* a control freak or something?"

"*Nee,* not at all. He knows a lot about horses and cares for them well, and he gave the girls instructions and they didn't follow them. He is the head of the household, so they should've listened to him."

"Do you listen to your *vadder* all the time?"

"*Jah,* I try to."

"That doesn't answer my question, Tulip. You mean to tell me you always do what your parents say like a good little girl?"

"Mostly."

Nathanial threw his head back and laughed. "That's

what I thought. What fun would we have if we obeyed our stuffy parents all the time?"

Tulip wasn't quite sure what he was getting at, or the point he was trying to make.

"So only one twin rode the horse too hard?"

"Jah."

"Do you realize you've just blamed both of them for that? You didn't name the twin, just said 'they.'"

"Oh."

"That's why I'm concerned that you've already done the same thing with me and my *bruder*. We're individuals you know."

"I know." Tulip realized he was right. Whenever one twin did anything wrong, she saw it as both of them. As though they came as a package. Anyway, Tulip had a sneaking suspicion that the twins never did anything without the other goading them on.

"Come on, stop pulling that face. The wind will change direction and your face will stay that way," he said as he leaned forward toward her, grinning.

The way he said it made Tulip laugh. Now she was certain he was a little devious as well as unreliable, but he was also a lot of fun to be around. And fun was probably what she was missing out on in life.

"That's better. You look so much more beautiful when you laugh, Tulip."

She looked down, embarrassment now heating her cheeks.

He leaned closer. "Hasn't anyone told you how beautiful you are?"

"I'm not used to people talking about such things as beauty."

"Well that's just nonsense in my opinion. If people can admire green fields, a beautiful sunset, a field of yellow corn, what's wrong with admiring a beautiful woman? *Gott* designed them all. They're all His handiwork."

"It's just that if people mention other people's looks in a positive manner, that person might get prideful if they think that they look beautiful. Anyway, that's just how I was raised. We don't give too many compliments in our household to guard against pride."

"I see your point. I won't tell you how much I like the color of your skin, or the way your eyes dance when you laugh, or how well your dark hair complements your eyes."

Tulip felt good about herself. It felt nice to hear all those things. "You know, saying that out loud is as good as telling me."

"*Gut,* because I wanted to let you know. You should know how beautiful you are, Tulip."

"Don't say that."

He laughed again. "Okay, I don't want to make you feel uncomfortable in any way."

"*Denke.*"

He shook his head. "Now if someone were to tell me I was the best looking man they'd ever seen, I'd be quite pleased with that."

Tulip giggled. "Are you fishing for compliments?"

"*Jah.*"

"And you think that's okay?" she asked.

He grinned and gave her a sharp nod.

"You certainly are very different from the men around here, Nathanial."

"Well, *denke.* That was your first compliment. See how easy that was?"

"Do you think it was, or was it an un-compliment? Something that was uncomplimentary is what I mean to say. You can't know what I think about the men around here. I could think the men around here are *wunderbaar* and since I just said that you're not like the men around here, perhaps I've just said something very awful to you."

"You're so smart, Tulip. I wouldn't have thought of any of that. Did you do well in *skul?*"

She shook her head. "There you go again."

He grinned cheekily. "Sorry, I just can't help myself, but that was genuine. I wasn't deliberately saying anything nice."

"So, the other things you were saying to me weren't genuine?"

"Tulip, you're tying me up in knots, and not in a good way. I mean everything I've ever said to you. You're smart and beautiful and that is a rare combination in a woman, and I don't care what you say. Someone needs to tell you the truth."

She looked down at her hands on her lap, not knowing what to say.

He chuckled again. "Aw, I've gone and embarrassed you now."

Tulip looked up at him. "I'm not embarrassed. I'm just not used to hearing such things."

"If I was your boyfriend, I would tell you that all the

time. I hope you give me that chance. Cancelling our buggy ride is not a good start to our relationship."

"I told you why I have to do that."

"Still, it's not a good sign for me. Men have feelings too. Some women are so worried about getting hurt that they hurt all the men around them."

She exhaled deeply. This wasn't as easy as she thought it was going to be. "I'm sorry."

His face lit up. "Will you make it up to me?"

Tulip didn't want to make a promise that she couldn't keep.

When she hesitated, he said, "You're not the only beautiful woman around here, Tulip."

Now Tulip felt like he was threatening her. If she didn't jump to his commands and do things when he wanted, he'd find someone else. It made her feel dreadful inside. She stood. "I'll talk to you later. I've got something I need to tell Chelsea that I forgot to tell her earlier."

"Wait! We haven't finished talking yet."

Tulip swung around to face him. "Our conversation has become uncomfortable. I'll talk to you later when you're in a better mood."

He called after her, "I don't know what you're talking about. It's you who's in the bad mood. You're the one walking away."

Acting like his words didn't bother her, Tulip kept walking. Even though he had said nice things, there was a definite sting to his words. Now Tulip was sure that he was saying things to her in order to gain control—the upper hand. Well, it wouldn't work with her.

. . .

WHEN TULIP BROUGHT the twins home that night, her mother pulled her into the kitchen. "Tulip, there is a man in this community called Wilhem Byler."

"I know, *Mamm*. I went to dinner with him on Monday night."

Her mother looked at her openmouthed and it took a few seconds before she could speak again. "Was that who you went with? I thought you said you went with girlfriends. You didn't tell me you went with a man. Were you deliberately keeping things from me? Was it a date?"

"Many couples keep their relationship a secret. I wasn't doing anything wrong. I don't have to tell you everything when I'm this age, do I? I'm old enough to be married and have my own family and my own home by now."

"Quite right. So it was a date, a proper date?"

After Tulip nodded, her mother took a few steps and glanced out at Tulip's father, who was still reading his newspaper on the couch in the living room.

"I didn't realize. That's *wunderbaar!*" her mother said, grinning from ear-to-ear.

"I'm glad you're happy about it, but why do you look so pleased? What do you know about him?" She had thought her mother would be annoyed with her for keeping things from her.

"One of my friends wrote me a letter about him. Wilhem's thinking of moving here and taking a *haus* with his cousin. He comes with the highest recommendations. Your *vadder* and I give our approval of him. Well, I mean, your *vadder* would if he knew about the whole thing."

Tulip put her fingertips to her mouth and giggled. "That's *gut!*"

"Is that all you have to say?"

"Jah." Tulip shrugged her shoulders. "What should I say?"

"Sit down," *Mamm* ordered. When they were both seated, her mother continued, "What's going on?"

"With Wilhem?"

"Jah."

"I really like him. He's so nice and gentle, and he seems sweet and kind."

"Gut! I'm happy about that."

"Can I go to bed now? It's been a long day and I had to stay there longer because the twins wanted to wait until everyone went home."

"Jah, of course."

Tulip hurried off to bed, wondering what developments might happen on Sunday, at the next community gathering. Nathanial had said he was going to introduce himself to her parents. What if he mentioned that she'd agreed to go on a date with him, or worse, told them they'd already been out together? And what if Wilhem found out? She had gotten herself into a complicated mess and she hoped and prayed that things would work out smoothly and no one would get hurt.

CHAPTER 14

When Tulip got to work the next day, Chelsea was waiting for her. As they readied things for their customers, Chelsea asked, "Why were you speaking to Nathanial so much last night? I thought you liked Wilhem."

"*Jah*, I do."

"You were talking and laughing with him. He looked like he was flirting with you."

"It was weird. It was a strange conversation." Tulip shook her head. "I can't even begin to tell you about it. The more time I spend with Nathanial the more odd I think he is. Don't tell anybody. I don't want people to think I'm gossiping."

"I won't. It's a shame. He's so handsome."

"He might be okay. I could be wrong about him. He might just be trying too hard or something like that."

"It's possible," Chelsea agreed.

"It can't be easy to come here, following his *bruder* being here."

"That's right."

Tulip took the chairs off the tables where they'd been stacked from the previous night's floor washing. Then she refilled the table shakers of their salt, pepper, and sugar, while Chelsea started up the coffee machine ready for their early morning breakfast crowd.

Not wanting to have her mind on Nathanial, when she had her next opportunity to talk with Chelsea, she asked her about Jonathan.

"Jonathan is great. I really like him."

"I'm glad. He's such a nice person. I'm glad you can see past his size. Oh, I don't mean anything rude by that."

"It's okay, I know what you mean. I've never been concerned with people's looks. It's the heart of the person that counts," Chelsea said.

When their boss walked in the back door, the two girls were quiet. Their boss didn't like them talking too much.

"Time to open the doors," Tulip said when she saw a regular customer by the door, waiting to get his regular take-out coffee. It was a few minutes before their official start time, but their boss was happy when the girls were ready early to open the doors for their customers.

CHAPTER 15

When Hezekiah Yoder stopped his buggy in the row with the other buggies on the Sunday morning, the twins were the first ones out.

Tulip got out next, and looked around. She had to avoid both Wilhem and Nathanial until things cooled down. Nathanial had been acting weird at the softball game and she hadn't seen him or heard from him since.

Tulip's parents were convinced she liked Wilhem, but what would they say about Nathanial? She sure hoped Nathanial would keep quiet.

She stuck close to her mother as she walked into the house where the Sunday morning meeting was being held.

As always, they were early. There were only two families who'd taken their seats in the house. Tulip's mother always sat at the front, while Tulip preferred to sit closer to the back. When her mother slid into the front row, Tulip headed to the back of the room where she'd soon be joined by Rose. She hadn't seen Rose for days and she wanted to tell her about the mess she'd gotten herself into. She hoped her big sister might be able to offer her a solution.

Ten minutes later, Rose and Mark came into the house. Tulip waved to Rose, and while Mark sat down with the men on one side of the room, Rose joined Tulip on the women's side. As was traditional at their Sunday meetings, men and women didn't sit together.

"Rose, I've got myself into a bit of a—well, it's a huge mess." Tulip managed to tell Rose the whole thing before the meeting began.

"You're worried about nothing, Tulip."

"Really?"

"Jah."

"I'm not sure who I like best, but I think that Wilhem's the best man for me."

"How are you judging that so early on?"

"Because Nathanial talked about a buggy ride and then I didn't see him for weeks. He was too casual about the whole thing. He seems to be the kind of man who doesn't follow through with things. Then at the baseball game he was acting weird and I thought he might be controlling. He was telling me I was beautiful and smart and giving me compliments. It just made me feel weird. I didn't like hearing it. I told him so and he wouldn't stop. Then I think he got a bit mean, unless I was judging what he said wrongly."

"I see your point. And you're worried that Wilhem might find out that you went out for coffee, or wherever you went, with Nathanial?"

Tulip nodded.

"You're worried about nothing. You're quite entitled to do that. You don't necessarily marry the first man you go on a buggy ride with—or on a date. Don't forget the same kind of thing happened with me. Mark was there the whole time watching me go out with Jacob. It couldn't have been easy for him, but he understood in the end."

"That's because you finally chose him."

"Well, my situation was a lot more complicated than your situation is."

"That's true." Breathing out heavily, Tulip felt the tension she'd been holding in her shoulders float away. Rose was right. Her situation had been dreadfully uncomfortable. "I've been so worried."

"Is there something else you're not telling me?" Rose peered into her face.

"*Nee*, not unless I've left something out that I don't remember. The only thing is that Wilhem asked me if I was going to the softball game and I said I didn't like softball. That was the game that Nathanial was supposed to be driving me home from. Do you see? Wilhem thought I wasn't going to it. What if he finds out that I was there? He lives with Jonathon, and he *was* there. What if Jonathon said something to him? He probably will and then when Wilhem will think I'm a dreadful liar." Her shoulders stooped. "Come to think of it, that's probably what I am."

Tulip nudged Rose when Wilhem walked into the house followed closely by Nathanial. "Look! There they are. Both of them."

"Nathanial looks an awful lot like Jacob. Wilhem looks

nice. If Wilhem asks why you were at the softball game, just say you had to drive the twins at the last minute."

"That would be lying. It's close to the truth, but not the truth."

"You could always tell the truth, then."

Tulip frowned. Lying wasn't a good idea and neither was telling the truth. "Telling the truth would be better, but what would that sound like? *Oh, Wilhem, before I knew you'd be back here, I accepted a buggy ride from another man I like, but since you've turned back up I got out of that and now I'm hoping he doesn't ask again or tell anyone we went out on a date because now I like you better."*

"*Jah,* that does sound bad, and kind of wacky," Rose agreed.

"I can't even explain myself. You see? Now I don't know what to do."

Rose and Tulip stopped their whispering and turned their eyes to the front when their father stood to open the meeting in prayer.

CHAPTER 16

*F*or the whole meeting, Tulip did her best to concentrate on what was being said. She didn't succeed very well, though, because she was too worried about what would happen afterward. What if both men approached her at the same time? She glanced over at Wilhem and Nathanial. Wilhem was sitting in the second row and Nathanial was sitting in the row directly behind him. What if the two men got to talking and her name came up? Her stomach churned at the thought.

When the meeting was over, Rose and Tulip stayed back until they were the last ones out of the house. After the Sunday meeting there was always food served. The men moved most of the long benches out of the house and replaced them with tables. In the warmer weather, the meal tables were set up in the yard.

"I'm going to help *Mamm* in the kitchen and hopefully avoid everyone," Tulip said.

"*Nee*, you shouldn't do that; not if you like Wilhem. You should go out and speak with him."

"I can speak to him later. Hopefully, when Nathanial's gone home."

"Don't let what happened between Jacob and me stop you from getting closer to Nathanial. He is not to be held responsible for his brother's shortcomings."

"I don't think I'm doing that. I'm not taking that into consideration at all."

Tulip headed back into the house and into the kitchen to help her mother and the other ladies with the food. Unfortunately, her mother kept giving her things to be taken outside even when she insisted she was happy to stay in the kitchen. Tulip went so far as to offer to do all the washing up as the dishes came back to the kitchen. Her mother wouldn't hear of it. It was as though her mother knew she wanted to hide away, and didn't want to help her do so.

When her mother loaded her up with bread to place on the tables, she saw Wilhem and to her amazement he headed straight to her.

"There you are."

She smiled at him, hoping he wasn't going to mention the softball game. Since he was smiling, it seemed like she was in the clear.

"How's everything going?" she asked as she placed one lot of bread on a table.

"I have some good news."

"What is it?" she asked.

By the smile on his face she thought it was something important

"Jonathon and I have found a nice *haus* to live in."

"That's *wunderbaar!* Is it close by? Wait, don't tell me

yet. Stay here for a minute while I put this bread out." She placed four lots of bread on four tables and headed back to Wilhem. "Tell me about it."

"It's the small place on the corner of this road just before the creek."

"I know the one; it's the white one with the red roof?"

"That's it."

"That's quite exciting."

"We're moving in there on Wednesday."

"That happened quickly."

"I tend to move fast when I know something is right."

He said it in a way that made her giggle.

"Could I drive you home after the singing tonight, Tulip?"

Tulip glanced around before she answered, hoping Nathanial was nowhere close. She saw Nathanial and her father talking. Both men were smiling and seemed to be getting along well.

"Tulip?"

She turned to face him. "I'm… I'm not staying for the singing tonight."

"Can I drive you home before that, then? Or how about I pick you up from work one day next week?"

Tulip smiled. That would be a better plan and less likely for the two men to run into each other. "I'd like that."

"Tuesday after you finish work?"

"Perfect."

He gave her a beaming smile. "I look forward to seeing you on Tuesday."

Tulip turned around to head back into the kitchen.

She had avoided a disaster, but now she wouldn't be able to stay on for the singing like she'd planned. That was a disappointment, but it would be worth it to avoid a disaster.

WHEN TULIP EMERGED from the kitchen after all the washing up had been done, she was relieved to see most of the people had gone home, leaving only the younger people who were staying for the singing. Thankfully, Nathanial was nowhere to be seen. She'd been successful at avoiding him—or so she had thought. As she was wiping the tables down before the men loaded them back onto the church wagon, he walked over to her.

"Have you been hiding from me?"

She smiled at him. "Of course not."

"That's what it seems like to me. Anyway, I spoke to your *vadder,* but I haven't been able to find your *mudder.*"

"She spends most of her time on Sundays in the kitchen organizing the food."

"I think your *vadder* likes me."

"I saw the two of you talking together. What did you say to him?"

"I just talked about a little of this, a little of that. He knows I'm Jacob's *bruder* and he didn't mind at all."

"I'm surprised you think that that would make a difference to anyone."

He shrugged his shoulders. "Well, you never know."

Seeing the men were loading the tables she'd wiped down, she moved on to the other tables while Nathanial followed her.

"Can I drive you home soon, Tulip?"

"Nee, I'm not staying for the singing."

"What about now?"

"I have to stay back and then go home with my *mudder."*

He nodded. "Are you playing hard-to-get?"

She turned around and stared at him, wondering if he was joking or whether he was serious. "I'm not playing anything."

He laughed and she laughed too. When she turned back to one of the tables, she felt someone was staring at her. She looked over her shoulder to see that it was Jonathon.

"I must help with the cleaning up of the kitchen," she said.

"I'm not giving up on you. I'll see you soon."

"Bye, Nathanial."

"I'll see you soon," he said again.

She hurried into the kitchen, worried about the way Jonathon had been staring at her. He had to know that there was something between her and Nathanial the way they were laughing together. Jonathon could easily say something about it to Wilhem.

Wilhem would think that she was the kind of girl who would date one man and date another man at the same time, and that was not who she was—not at all. It concerned her that she liked both men.

CHAPTER 17

"*I*'ve been spending time with Jonathon," Chelsea said at work the next day.

"And?" Tulip asked. "I already know you like one another. We have talked about it." Chelsea had spoken as though she'd never mentioned Jonathan before.

"He's surprisingly mature. He knows some people laugh about him and his weight and it doesn't bother him. He's got a health condition and he ballooned up when he took the medication to keep it under control."

"Really? I didn't know he was sick."

"I know; neither did I. He wasn't always the size he is and I never knew why he suddenly gained weight."

"I feel awful. I had no idea."

Chelsea leaned in and whispered, "I like him as more than friends."

"You do? That's fantastic. He's such a nice man."

"He is, and he's so gentle and warm-hearted."

Tulip felt all warm and fuzzy. She was glad she

might've played a small part in the two of them finding love with each other.

"What's happening with Wilhem?"

She shook her head. "I'm not sure. I'm going out with him tomorrow night. He's picking me up from here."

"That's good, isn't it?"

"Normally it would be, but I can't help worrying because I went out with Nathanial Schumacher once and he thinks I like him, and, well, maybe I do, but not as much as Wilhem."

"I see. You like both of them for different reasons."

"I guess, but Wilhem seems to be the more reliable one. I didn't tell you I liked Nathanial before because I didn't want to tell anyone."

"Are you choosing Wilhem because he's reliable, or does your heart tell you that he's the one you want?"

She shook her head. "Why is everything so complicated?"

"It's not. It shouldn't be."

"My *mudder* says a woman should choose a man with her head and not her heart," Tulip said.

"You're the one who has to live with your choice, so just be sure you choose right."

Tulip giggled. *"Denke,* but that was no help at all."

"I'm not your *mudder,*" Chelsea said with a grin. "Shh. Here comes Audrey."

Both girls stopped talking when their boss came into the bakery.

~

LATER THAT NIGHT, Tulip was sitting with her family around the dinner table.

"We met a new man today," Daisy said. "He said you know him, Tulip."

"Who is he?"

"His name is Nathanial Schumacher," Daisy replied.

Tulip gulped. She hadn't given the slightest thought to one of her sisters snatching away a man she liked. But she hadn't given him any encouragement yesterday when he wanted to drive her home.

Their mother dropped her fork onto her plate when she heard the man's name. "Where did you meet him?"

"At the supermarket."

Mr. Yoder frowned at his wife. "You let them go alone?"

"I thought they should start to take on some small responsibilities since they're getting older."

"We didn't have one accident with the buggy," Lily added. "We drove slow and the horse is fine."

"We hitched it and unhitched it by ourselves and rubbed the horse down and everything just like you showed us."

Their father scratched his beard in an agitated manner. "I suppose that's progress."

"Anyway, Nathanial's very nice. I thought we might be able to have him over for dinner one night," Daisy said.

Lily added, "Along with his cousin, Matthew Schumacher, because he's staying at Matthew's place."

Tulip stared at their mother. She knew *Mamm* liked Matthew because her oldest daughter was married to Mark, Matthew's older brother.

"We'll see." Mrs. Yoder picked up her fork and started eating.

"*Mamm,* you always say that when you mean 'no' and don't want to say it," Daisy said.

"Since *Dat* is the deacon, I think it's only reasonable to welcome visitors and newcomers to the community by having them over for dinner," Lily said.

Their father leaned back in his chair and stared at Lily, who was sitting next to him. "And since when have you developed this sense of what a deacon should do?"

Lily shrugged. "I've been watching my lovely *vadder* and how nice and hospitable he's always been to everyone."

Mr. Yoder laughed, while his wife was glaring at Daisy, the twin who'd raised the subject of Nathanial Schumacher.

He glanced at his wife's stern face. "It's your *mudder* who runs the *haus.* She has the say on the matter."

"And, as I already said, we'll see." Her tone was firm.

"Well, that makes things kind of awkward," Daisy said.

"Why?" Mrs. Yoder asked.

"We already invited them to dinner. They're coming on Wednesday night."

Tulip looked on in silence as their mother reprimanded the twins.

"Is there something you don't like about them, *Mamm?*" Daisy asked. "We always have people over for the evening meal. And many people drop by without being invited."

"Yeah, *Mamm.* Why are you like this about Nathanial and Matthew?"

She shook her head. "It's nothing. I've got no problem with either of them. Of course I don't."

"So, it's all right for Wednesday night?" Daisy asked.

"It would be embarrassing if we had to cancel," Lily added.

"*Nee,* you can't cancel. It'll be okay." She glanced at her husband and he remained silent.

IN HER ROOM later that night, Tulip was worried. Had Nathanial somehow gotten the twins to invite him because he liked her, or was it one of the twins he was interested in? What would happen when Wilhem found out that Nathanial had been invited to her house, but he hadn't been invited?

Tulip changed into her nightgown and ripped off her prayer *kapp* and threw it on her nightstand. Without brushing out her hair, she slipped between the covers.

Tossing and turning, many solutions traveled through her mind. Perhaps she should invite Wilhem as well? But then he'd be sure to find out that she'd been out with Nathanial.

One thing was for certain, if she found out that Nathanial was using the twins to get to her, she'd be mighty annoyed. She knew by the way the twins had been talking that one of them liked him.

CHAPTER 18

Tulip waited outside the cake store after closing on Tuesday for Wilhem to take her on their date. It wasn't long before she saw a buggy heading toward her. It was Wilhem driving it.

"Hello," she said as she climbed into the buggy.

"Hello."

"Where are we off to?"

"It's a surprise."

He didn't have to do anything special. She just liked to spend time with him and that would've been enough. But it sounded too gooey to tell him that, so she stayed silent.

"It's not too much of a surprise. I've just picked up the keys for the *haus*. I thought I'd take you there first and show you through it. I would've cooked you dinner, but there's no furniture there yet."

"That's exciting. When do you move in?"

"Tomorrow."

"I'm sorry, I missed that—you can cook?"

"Yeah. Why's that so surprising? I can do lots of things.

I can even sew, and what's more it was my *grossdaddi* who showed me how to sew. He told me that he was out in the fields one day and cut himself on some wire. There were no hospitals in those days, not close by anyway. He either had to sew the cut closed or bleed to death. So, he sewed the cut shut."

"Ooohh! That's an awful story. I'm glad you didn't tell me that while we were eating. Yuck!"

Wilhem laughed. "Awful maybe, but it's true."

"And that's why he thought you should learn to sew? In case you cut yourself open?"

"Not exactly. Things like that do come in handy, though. Mind you, I didn't say I was a good cook, I just said I could cook. I'm not good at sewing either."

Tulip laughed.

He stopped the buggy close to the house. "We've still got some daylight left."

HE SHOWED Tulip through the small house that he was going to share with his cousin, Jonathon. Wilhem was acting like he hadn't heard anything about the friendly way she'd been speaking with Nathanial on the Sunday just gone and Tulip couldn't have been more relieved.

The house had only two bedrooms, one bathroom, a kitchen, and one living area. It was small but cozy. The living room and the kitchen were floored with gray slate tiles.

"It's nice. I think you'll be happy here."

"I'm sure we will be. Now let's have dinner."

He'd booked a table at an Italian restaurant in town.

They had to travel back along the roads they'd just traveled down.

"I'm glad you like it here in this county, Wilhem."

"I do. There seems to be so much more happening here than back home."

"I've only ever lived here."

"Trust me, it's a nice place to live. And I've got work lined up for the next three months."

"I'm happy for you."

He smiled at her and when their eyes met, she knew she'd made the right decision, choosing him over Nathanial.

Once they'd parked the buggy close to the restaurant, they walked up the road together. The chill of the night air bit into her cheeks, causing her to shiver.

"Are you cold?" he asked.

"Not too cold."

When they arrived at the restaurant, he moved forward and held the door open for her so she could walk through first. She thanked him as she walked through the doorway. Once they were inside, they were greeted by a waiter who showed them to their table in the corner of the dimly lit room. William moved quickly to pull the chair out for her. He was being completely chivalrous and doing all the right things.

Two pink roses sat in the center of the table and in front of them a white candle flickered.

When he sat down opposite, Tulip said, "This is so nice and lovely."

He gave her a big smile. "You haven't even tried the food yet."

"I know I'll like it. I like the feel of the place."

"*Gut.* I'm glad you like it."

Soft music played in the background, creating a romantic mood.

"Do you think will be able to see our food? It's kind of dark in here."

"Will we be able to read the menus?" Tulip asked.

Wilhem looked over at the approaching waiter holding two menus. "It looks like we'll soon find out."

Tulip ordered salad and lasagna, figuring it would be easier to eat than spaghetti, which she'd probably have trouble getting onto a fork. Wilhem ordered the seafood pasta. For drinks they both opted for soda.

"Tell me more about yourself," Tulip said.

"You probably already know more about me than most people do. Even my own parents."

Tulip giggled. "I don't think that would be true."

"Well, what would you like to know specifically?"

"What are your hopes for the future?"

"I'd like to get married and have a large *familye.* Isn't that what everyone wants?"

"I guess so."

"What about you?"

"I want to get married and have a family as well. I would like to have an interesting life. Maybe I'd like to travel and see places."

"What kind of places?"

"I don't know. I just want to do something a little bit different."

He slowly nodded. "You don't want to be the same as everybody else?"

Tulip giggled. "You're probably right."

The waiter brought their drinks and warm bread, and told them their food wouldn't be long. Tulip was so hungry she felt like eating all the bread, but then she knew she wouldn't have room for the main meal.

She wondered if it might be best to come right out and say something to Wilhem about the softball game and Nathanial, but as she'd discussed with Rose, it would sound too strange. She didn't want Wilhem to think she was a strange girl.

Wilhem picked up the bread and offered it to her. "Would you like some?"

"Just a little bit." She broke off a small piece.

"Butter?"

She shook her head and then watched as he took a large slice of bread and scraped a great deal of butter on it.

"I see you like a little bit of bread with your butter."

He laughed. "I've always loved butter. Everything is always better with butter."

Tulip giggled. "I can't believe you just said that."

"It's true."

There was a moment of silence while they both ate the bread

"I've noticed that Jonathan and Chelsea are getting along well."

"*Jah*, they are."

"Jonathan tells me that you helped him. You put in a good word for him."

"I don't know if that did any good."

"I think it did and so does Jonathan, so *denke*."

"You are most welcome, if I did anything to help. I've always liked Jonathan. Chelsea tells me he's got something happening with his health?"

Wilhem nodded. "He likes to keep that quiet because he doesn't want to be seen or treated as the sick person."

"I can understand that. I haven't told anyone and I won't tell anyone."

"Good." He finished eating his bread and butter.

They were getting along so well, but every now and again she was reminded that it could all end quickly if Wilhem found out she'd lied to him about being at the softball game. Rose had told her not to worry, but it was hard not to.

Their main meals arrived, taking her mind off her concerns.

"Yours looks nice," he said.

"So does yours," she said, studying his seafood. It had been a while since she'd enjoyed seafood. That's what she should've ordered.

"Do you want to swap?"

She giggled. "How about we go halves?"

"Half each?"

"Jah."

"Good idea."

She cut her lasagna down the middle and moved one half of it onto his plate. Then he gave her half his seafood pasta.

"The best of both worlds," he said.

"That's a bit dramatic. It's just food."

"I love food."

"Ah, now I am learning more about you. I've learned that you love butter and you also love food."

"That's right."

"Italian food in particular?"

"All kinds of food and I hope you're a good cook."

"Of course I am. I love cooking."

"That fits well because I love eating."

It was a silly conversation, but just being with him, talking about nothing in particular, made Tulip happier than she'd been in a long time. Her stress of earlier in the evening faded away.

When they finished their meals, Wilhem asked, "Dessert?"

Tulip patted her stomach. "I couldn't possibly, but you have some if you want. They might be able to bring you some more butter with a spoon."

He laughed at her. "I'll give dessert a miss if you aren't going to have any with me."

"Are you trying to make me feel guilty?"

He leaned over, close to her. "Is it working?

"*Nee*, it's not. There's nothing you could say that would make me be able to fit anything else in."

He chuckled. "Okay, but I'm not ready to go home yet. I'll keep you for a little longer, if that's all right with you."

"It is."

They talked easily for another hour and Tulip was pleased at how well they were getting along.

When they both noticed other people in the restaurant leaving, Wilhem said, "I should be getting you home, or your parents will be worried."

"Okay. *Denke* for a lovely dinner."

"Does that mean you'll go out with me again?"

"I will."

"That makes me happy."

As they walked to the buggy, Tulip again became worried about Nathanial. She felt that she might be sitting on a volcano that was about to erupt and she didn't want to lose Wilhem. She liked him even more after tonight.

Tulip shrugged off her fears and enjoyed the romantic walk beside the attractive man as they walked up the street in the chilly night air.

"I had the best night I've ever had," he said, glancing down at her.

"I've really enjoyed it too." It would've been the best night she'd had if she hadn't been so worried about what the future might hold.

When he stopped the buggy in front of her home, Tulip waited, hoping he'd make definite plans to see her again.

"I don't want the night to end. I'd like it if we could turn time back and start from the beginning and do tonight all over again."

Tulip laughed. He was a little silly and so carefree. She loved his easy manner.

"Would you care to come on a buggy ride with me on Friday night?" he asked.

"Jah, I'd like that."

"Shall I collect you at eight?"

She stared at him in the semi-darkness. The only light was coming from inside the house. "That sounds *gut.*"

"Perfect."

Tulip climbed down from the buggy and before she got to the front door of her house, Wilhem had turned the buggy to face the road. Now the buggy was still. She turned when she got to the door and waved to him. When she saw that he waved back, she opened the door and stepped through. No one would be able to ruin how she felt, not the twins, not anyone. She felt so happy inside that she felt she might burst. She'd found her perfect man just like Rose had found hers.

She hung her shawl on the peg by the door and had expected to be faced with the twins asking her how her night had gone. Rather than the twins running up to her, it was her mother.

"I'm so glad you're home." Tulip's mother took her by the hand and dragged her into the kitchen. "I've been so worried and you weren't here for me to talk with. I'm so glad you're home."

"What is it?"

"The twins."

"I guessed it was something about one of them. What have they done now?" It would be just like the twins to ruin her slim chance of happiness.

"Nothing lately. It's just that I'm worried about Nathanial coming here. They knew I wouldn't want him here and that's why they didn't ask me first. You heard, didn't you, about Jacob?"

"*Jah*, but that's Jacob and not Nathanial."

"They're part of the same seed."

Tulip pulled her mouth to one side. "I don't think that's fair, *Mamm*."

"I've seen it before. Children of the same *familye*

generally do the same things because they've got the same morals."

"I don't think that's what happened. Jacob, and the girl he ended up marrying, made a mistake, but they made it right. Shouldn't people's sins be forgotten? *Gott* forgets them. Besides, don't forget that Nathanial and Jacob are cousins of Mark and Matthew, and there's nothing wrong with them. You allowed Mark to marry Rose."

"Generally you'd be right, but we're talking about the twins. I don't want to see them get into any trouble. I worry about them. They're too flighty and headstrong for their own good and they're immature—far too immature for their age."

"They'll be all right. They just need some time to grow up."

"But they're already keeping company with people like Nathanial Schumacher."

"You should be glad they asked the boys here to dinner; they aren't sneaking off somewhere with them."

Mrs. Yoder's face suddenly brightened. "You're right. I didn't see it like that. I feel much better now. Maybe I've been wrong about Nathanial. Your *vadder* said he seemed nice."

"You should know more about him by the end of dinner on Wednesday."

"You're right. *Denke,* Tulip." Her mother stood up and kissed her on her forehead. "I feel so much better. *Gut nacht.*" Mrs. Yoder hurried out of the room.

Tulip sat there alone at the kitchen table, thinking about what she'd just heard. She was more certain than ever that Nathanial had forced the invitation for dinner.

Her mother had been so worried about the twins and Nathanial that she hadn't even asked how Tulip's time with Wilhem had gone.

When she had time to sit there and think things through, she realized she'd just made a big mistake. She had the opportunity to change her mother's mind about having Nathanial there. He could've possibly been uninvited and that would've been a good thing. Why did she defend him when he could very well ruin everything for her?

CHAPTER 19

On Wednesday night, Tulip decided she should have a quiet word with Nathanial before he came inside the house. That way she could possibly diffuse a bad situation before it happened. She watched the driveway from the living room so she could be first outside to speak with him. The twins were in the kitchen helping their mother with dinner when a buggy pulled up. Tulip raced outside and met Nathanial as he jumped out of the buggy. She looked around for Matthew.

"Hello, Nathanial. Where's Matthew?"

"He was working late, or doing something for his *vadder*. He'll be along soon. He told me to go ahead and get here first."

"I see. I wanted to talk with you about something so it worked out well that Matthew didn't come with you."

He drew his eyebrows together. "Wilhem? Is that why you didn't want me to take you home on Sunday?"

Tulip froze. "What do you know about Wilhem?"

"I know enough."

Tulip hated confrontation and didn't know what to say. "I was put in an awkward situation."

"And what was that?" He folded his arms across his chest. She shook her head and opened her mouth to speak and he butted in, "You've been two-timing me?"

Tulip frowned. That's what she'd been afraid of all along. She wasn't a two-timer but now people would think that she was. "I'm not. It just happened like that. I wasn't seeing you both at the same time. It was nothing like that."

"You led me to believe that you would be seeing me in the future at some point." He walked up close to her and, he being taller, she only came up to his chin. "Are you telling me that you've chosen Wilhem over me?"

"I haven't, I ... er ..."

"Haven't you heard about him?"

Tulip looked into his face and wondered why she'd ever found him handsome. Right now, his personality overshadowed his looks and he was anything but attractive. "What do you mean?"

"That's why Wilhem had to move here."

"Why?"

"*Nee!* I'm not going to be a talebearer. You can find that out for yourself."

Nathanial took a large stride to walk into her house, but she stepped in front of him to block his way.

"What is there to find out? He said he likes it better here and he's found work," Tulip said.

He shook his head at her. "You people gave my *bruder* such a hard time when he was here."

"Who did?"

"Never mind." He took a giant sideways step and walked past her into her house.

Now she'd have to sit through an awkward dinner with a man who'd been so horrible to her. And what if he'd said something to Wilhem about her? Tulip wasn't certain whether he knew something dreadful about Wilhem or whether he was just trying his best to make him seem like a bad choice. Besides, how would Nathanial know anything about him since they didn't even belong to the same community?

Now Tulip felt sick to her stomach. She shouldn't have rushed out to meet him. She didn't want to join them for dinner, but she had no choice.

THROUGHOUT THE DINNER, every time Tulip glanced up from her plate, she could see Nathanial scowling at her. It was plain to see that she'd hurt his feelings. As for Matthew, he seemed unaware of the tension between Nathanial and herself.

She wondered if Matthew was interested in one of the twins. She noticed his eyes kept glancing in Daisy's direction while Daisy had her eyes fixed on Nathanial. It would be her mother's worst nightmare-come-true if Daisy liked Nathanial. To be on the safe side, Tulip kept out of the dinner conversation as best she could, only speaking when she was spoken to.

When everyone finished dinner, it was time for coffee in the living room. Wanting to be on her own, Tulip volunteered to make the coffee, even telling her mother to go out and join their guests.

Just when she was in the middle of pouring the coffee into the cups, Nathanial came into the kitchen. She glanced at him and said nothing.

"Were you stringing me along in case things didn't work out with someone else?" he asked her.

"It was nothing like that." She shook her head. "Nothing like that at all. Let me explain."

"Why would I listen to a liar like you?"

Tulip gasped. No one had ever spoken so rudely to her, not even her twin sisters. "If you think I'm a liar, why are you here having dinner at my *haus?* It's not nice to call me a liar in my own home."

"Would it be better to call you a liar outside the *haus?* Do you want to talk about this outside right now?"

"Shh! Someone will hear you."

"I don't mind if they do; then you can explain to them what you've done."

"You didn't answer my question. Why are you here?" She had to find out if he liked one of the twins, or whether he was just using them to get to her.

"Lily and Daisy asked Matthew and me to dinner. It would've been rude to say no, wouldn't it?"

"You could've easily refused."

He laughed in a cruel manner.

"Everything all right in here?"

They both turned to see Mrs. Yoder standing by the door with her hands on her hips.

"I just came here to help Tulip carry the coffee out," he said.

Tulip said nothing and walked past him with coffee cups on a tray.

"Stop, Tulip. Let me do that." He walked forward and grabbed the tray from her so forcefully she had no choice but to let go.

Once Nathanial was clear of the kitchen, her mother asked, "What's really going on here, Tulip?"

"Nothing, nothing at all."

"I don't believe that. There is something going on between the two of you. Tell me—what is it?"

"I'll tell you when everyone goes home."

Her mother tilted her head. "So, there is something?"

"It's nothing much, really," Tulip said as she moved past her mother.

The boys only stayed for one cup of coffee. It was Matthew who suggested they go. Maybe he had sensed that something wasn't quite right.

When they left, the twins raced up to their rooms. Their father went to bed, while Tulip and her mother headed into the kitchen to wash the dinner dishes.

Tulip turned on the hot water tap and shook the soap in the holder to create the soapy washing up water.

"Do I have to drag it out of you?" Her mother placed a pile of dishes on the edge of the sink.

Tulip turned off the tap. "I wasn't going to tell you. I went out with Nathanial once, a while ago, for a cup of coffee. It was no big deal."

Her mother's jaw dropped open in shock. "Why didn't you tell me?"

"It was nothing. Except I agreed to go on a buggy ride with him and then nothing happened. He went away for weeks and came back as though nothing had happened and then said he wanted me to go on a buggy ride again, but by that time, I'd met Wilhem."

"The one you went out to dinner with? *Jah,* I like *him.*"

"I know you don't like Nathanial so that's why I didn't say anything. Anyway, now Nathanial is upset that I like Wilhem, or something. He said I two-timed him. I don't know how he found out about Wilhem."

"Someone would've told him. News always gets out. People like to talk about others."

Tulip sighed. "I know. Someone would've seen us together, I suppose."

Her mother tapped her chin. "I'm confused. Does he like either of the twins, or you?"

"I don't know. I was worried he might be using the twins to get back at me. Maybe I'm worrying about nothing and I don't want you to think the worst about him. I could be wrong." Tulip pushed the dirty plates under the water.

"Do the twins know what happened between the two of you?"

"*Nee,* I've not said anything to them."

"I think we should keep this between ourselves, don't you?"

"Okay, *Mamm.* I feel better now that you know. I've told Rose, but she won't say anything to anyone."

"If you've told Rose, you should've told me. You should never keep anything from me."

Tulip turned and smiled at her mother, feeling better that she'd told her the whole story. "The only thing I'm worried about is if Nathanial says something to Wilhem about me. He could talk to him alone and he might say that we were dating."

"He wouldn't say that if it wasn't true. You can't worry about that."

"I do, though. And it's making me feel sick whenever I think about it."

"Well, there's an easy cure for that."

"Don't think about it?" Tulip asked, predicting what her mother was about to say.

"Exactly."

It was a hard thing to do. Where would she find another nice man like Wilhem if things went sour between them?

CHAPTER 20

*T*ulip spent the rest of the time leading up to Friday night worried about Wilhem, and was continually fearful that he might find out about her spending time with Nathanial. She figured the only thing she could do was come clean to him and tell him what had happened.

A little before eight, she heard the buggy coming toward the house.

The twins had been unusually quiet that evening, and had been like that ever since Nathanial and Matthew's visit to the house. They hadn't even teased Tulip about going on a buggy ride. There was something going on with them and Tulip knew she'd have to find out what it was, but first she had to tell Wilhem what had been troubling her.

When she climbed into the buggy, she got the fright of her life. Instead of seeing Wilhem, it was Nathanial. She blinked hard, thinking that the semi-darkness might be playing tricks on her eyes. It was definitely Nathanial.

"What are you doing here?" she hissed.

"I told Wilhem what you were like and he said he no longer wanted anything to do with you."

"Why would you do that?"

He laughed. "It was my duty to tell my *bruder* in the Lord what he was getting himself in for."

"You had no right to interfere. Anyway, I was going to tell him what happened."

"Little late now."

She glared at him. "Why are you here?"

"To deliver the message."

"What message?"

"Wilhem's message that he wants nothing more to do with you."

She made to get out of the buggy, but he grabbed her arm.

"Let go, Nathanial! You're hurting me!"

"Wilhem can't find forgiveness in his heart for you, but maybe I can."

"I haven't done anything wrong."

"You're delusional."

"You're so rude!"

He laughed, and he still had a firm grip on her arm. "Look at things this way. Come on a buggy ride with me, or explain to your *familye* why Wilhem no longer wants to see you."

"That would be easier than explaining why I went on a buggy ride with you and not Wilhem. I thought you liked one of the twins."

"I could have either of them. They both like me."

She jumped out of the buggy, ripping her arm out of

his grasp as she did so. He jumped out of the buggy, caught up with her, and swung her around to face him.

"What you're saying is you prefer Wilhem?"

"*Jah,* I do."

"Well, too bad that's not going to happen now, but I'm still here, willing to forgive and forget."

She pushed him away and ran to the house, slamming the door behind her. Everyone was in the living room sitting around the fire and their heads turned to stare at her.

"What's wrong, Tulip?" her father said, bounding to his feet.

She kept back the tears that were threatening to spill from her eyes. "Nothing. I feel a little ill so I thought I should stay inside tonight. It's too cold out."

When her father sat down, Tulip raced to the kitchen. When she looked out the window, she saw that the buggy had gone. She sat down at the table, glad that Nathanial had gone. Tears ran down her face. Wilhem didn't want anything to do with her. Amish men chose their wives carefully and now he thought Tulip was a different kind of woman from the one that she was.

She quickly wiped her face with the end of her apron when she heard people heading to the kitchen. It was the twins.

"What's wrong, Tulip?" Daisy asked as she pulled out a chair to sit next to her.

She shook her head. "Nothing."

"Why did you come back inside so fast? You were looking forward to seeing Wilhem." Lily stood behind Daisy.

"It's complicated."

"Did you have a fight, or an argument?" Lily asked.

"Something like that. Make me a cup of tea?"

"I'll do it," Lily said.

"What's going on with the two of you? We haven't talked for a while," Tulip said.

Tulip and the twins sat, drank tea, and talked. Neither of the twins mentioned Nathanial—to Tulip's relief.

IT WAS Sunday meeting when Tulip saw Wilhem again. He caught her eye and to her surprise, he smiled and gave her a wave. She waved back. He didn't seem upset at all. Then he walked over to her. Perhaps he was a man who would forgive her.

What if she had been the reason he moved all that way and moved in with Jonathon? She half thought she might be the reason he'd moved away from his family and now he could be mightily disappointed and she couldn't blame him. She wished she had never laid eyes on Nathanial, but it was too late for that now.

"Are you feeling better, Tulip?" he asked with concern in his eyes.

"What do you mean?"

"You were sick on Friday and had to miss our buggy ride." Seeing her blank face, he added, "Didn't you send Matthew and his cousin to the house to tell me that?"

Tulip put the pieces together. Wilhem still knew nothing about what had happened between her and Nathanial. Nathanial had successfully ruined her planned time alone with Wilhem by telling him she was sick. He must've learned about her Friday-night date from the twins—that's all she could figure. The twins weren't good at keeping quiet about things.

"Not exactly," she said. "I didn't send them to the *haus* and I wasn't sick."

He drew his eyebrows together. "What do you mean?"

"It's a long story."

"Perhaps you can tell me about it over a walk with me in the park this afternoon?"

Tulip smiled. "I'd like that."

"How about we skip the singing? I'm too old for it anyway."

"Okay." Tulip looked around. "I better help *Mamm* now or I won't be going anywhere."

"I'll be here when you're ready to leave."

Tulip hurried away and left him standing there.

She was pleased that she'd have a chance to tell him the truth rather than him hearing half-truths from someone else. The only drawback to their time together that afternoon would be that she would have to tell him that she hadn't told the complete truth about the softball game that Wednesday night a couple of weeks back. And also that she had made the plans to go on the buggy ride before she saw him again. She hoped he would take the news well. At least she would no longer be lying.

CHAPTER 21

*W*ilhem had chosen a deserted spot in a field for their time alone together. He spread out a blanket next to a patch of wildflowers.

"It's beautiful here."

He looked around. "It is. Now, what did you have to tell me? You've been quiet all the way here in the buggy."

She gulped and looked around, wondering how to begin. "A picnic with no food?"

He laughed. "It was a little short notice. Next time, I'll be prepared."

"I think we've both had enough to eat anyway."

"I know I have," he said. "I think it's the company that creates a picnic. And right now, I'm having a happy time being with you. Now, tell me what's troubling you."

She took a deep breath. "Long before I knew you, well, days before I met you, I had coffee with Nathanial. I then agreed to go on a buggy ride with him later, but I heard nothing and forgot about it. Then I met you. Later, Nathanial came back expecting me to go on that buggy ride and by then I'd agreed to go out with you." She held her head and laughed when she saw him smirking. "It's not funny. I think that's what happened. It's confusing."

"I know I'm confused."

She looked into his brown eyes. "I wanted you to know what happened in case ... well, in case you heard the story a different way than how it happened because I didn't want to go out with him after I met you. Then things became awkward between Nathanial and me."

"I'm pleased that you told me."

"You don't think badly of me?"

"I can't think why I would. You're not tied to a man just because you agree to go on a buggy ride or you have a cup of coffee with him."

Tulip's body relaxed and she let go of the breath she'd been holding onto. "I thought you might think me a two-timer."

He laughed. "Not at all. That's a silly thing to think. I'm glad you prefer me. It makes me feel good to know that my feelings for you are returned."

Tulip hadn't foreseen things going so well. She hadn't wanted to reveal to him she had feelings for him, but it had turned out for the best because now he'd admitted he liked her. "That's such a relief."

He frowned. "Is there something you're not telling me?"

"*Nee,* I've told you everything. Except, I didn't tell you that I wasn't sick on Friday night. Nathanial made that up. He came to collect me and I got into the buggy thinking that it was your buggy. I couldn't see in the darkness until I was sitting beside him."

"That's deceitful of him." He shook his head and pressed his lips firmly together, and then he asked, "Why would he do that?"

"He wanted to ruin things between us. He told me outright that you didn't want to see me anymore and he said that he told you I was a two-timer."

"Ah, that's why you were a little nervous with me earlier today."

Tulip nodded. "I didn't know then that he had been lying about what he'd told me in the buggy."

He took his hat off to run his large hand through his sandy-colored hair. "It's quite shocking that he'd do that."

"I know. It was awful."

"So, he did that hoping you'd forget about me and go on the buggy ride with him?"

Tulip shrugged her shoulders. "I guess so. *Nee*, come to think of it, the way he was acting he wouldn't have expected me to go out with him. I think he was getting back at me for rejecting him."

"That sounds more like it." He put his hat back on. "At least now the truth is out in the open. Don't ever be afraid to tell me anything, Tulip."

"I won't. It sounded too silly to tell you everything at the start, but I didn't know it was going to blow up." She ran her hand over the delicate yellow wildflowers.

"Things tend to do that sometimes."

"It just got so complicated and I would rather be with you."

"I understand. Don't be upset."

Tulip could barely look at him and blinked back tears,

not wanting to cry in front of him. "I feel better now that I've told you."

"He made you feel bad for no reason. Forget it and forget about him."

Tulip nodded. "I will."

"Are you sure you're okay? Look at me."

Tulip took her gaze away from the flowers and looked into his face.

"Everything's fine."

"I hope you don't think less of me now or think that I'm immature."

"If anything I think more of you. What you've just told me shows me what a caring and sensitive person you are."

"Really?"

"Jah." He put himself to his feet and held out his hand. "Let's go for a walk while the sun is still smiling down on us."

Tulip gave a little giggle at his words and reached her hand up. He pulled her to her feet. "Where are we going?" she asked, pleased that he still had hold of her hand.

"Nowhere in particular."

"That sounds good to me."

He looked down at her and smiled. She knew from the way he looked at her with softness in his eyes that he really liked her. They walked through a clump of trees. "I think there should be a creek along here."

"There is. I'm sure."

Tulip heard the running water before she saw it. There was no path running by the water, only thick trees growing from the water's edge and continuing along the banks.

"It doesn't look like a nice stretch of water. I was hoping we could walk along the side," Wilhem said.

"How about we walk up further and see if it gets any better?"

"Okay."

Tulip didn't care where they walked or what they did. She was just pleased to be with him and he was still holding her hand. They walked on, following the water for another fifteen minutes.

"I think we should go somewhere for a cup of coffee. Somewhere where we can sit down on a chair."

Tulip laughed. "That sounds good."

"Are you getting hungry?"

"Mmm, I'm starting to get hungry."

"Me too. Let's go." He swung her around and they headed back to his buggy. "Do you know any good food places?" he asked once they were in the buggy and he had hold of the reins.

"There's a diner just up this road a little way."

"How's the food?"

"Quite good from memory. I haven't been there in some time. I went there with Rose just before she got married."

"That wasn't long ago. This way?" He nodded his head to the left.

"That's right, and then left again at the crossroads, and then you'll run into it on the right hand side of the road. You can't miss it."

"That's what people always say. It's easy when you know where something is. I'm not good with directions."

"Just as well I know where it is. Most men aren't good with directions."

He pulled a face at her. "I'm not most men."

"Well, like I said, a lot of them aren't good with directions and neither are you. What does that tell you?"

He frowned. "I'm not sure. Nothing?" He clicked his horse forward. "I'll have you know that I'm different from other men."

"How so?"

His brow scrunched and he took a while to answer. "I don't know," he finally said as his face relaxed into a smile. "I was trying to impress you, and then I didn't have anything intelligent to say to follow it with."

Tulip giggled at him. She liked the way he was so relaxed and wasn't afraid to be silly. "You remind me a little of Mark, my new *bruder*-in-law."

"Ah, that's a *gut* thing?" He glanced at her.

"It is."

"And in what way do I remind you of him?"

"Just your easy-going manner. You're so calm and relaxed—easy to be around."

"I'm happy to hear it."

"I really miss her Rose. It feels strange to be in the *haus* without her. We used to do everything together. She was like my best friend."

"My *vadder* used to say that the one thing we can be sure of in life is change."

"That sounds like something my *vadder* would say, but he'd mention sailing down a river and he'd talk about the changing currents to go along with it."

"They sound similar, our two *vadders*."

"*Jah*. They do, but yours is right about change. Things are always changing whether we want them to or not. When each of my *bruders* got married and left the *haus*, things weren't the same, but it didn't matter so much because I was so close with Rose and now she's gone. It's like a part of me has left. I know that sounds dramatic, but it's so quiet at home without her."

"You were closest with her out of all your sisters?"

"*Jah*. The twins are practically inseparable, so it was always the twins and then there was Rose and me."

He stopped the buggy at the diner. "I'm close with all my siblings equally. I don't know why. We're all spread out in ages so maybe that's why."

"Could be." Tulip got out of the buggy and watched as Wilhem secured his horse.

THEY SAT in a booth looking at the menu. "What will you have, Tulip? My treat."

"*Nee*, it's my treat this time."

"*Nee* it's not. I'll pay."

"I work. I can afford it."

He chuckled. "That's not the point. I refuse to let you pay and that's that." He closed the menu and then snatched hers out of her hand.

She looked across at him in shock and saw his smiling face. "Okay, you can pay. Just give me back the menu."

He handed it back to her. "Now, what looks good?" he asked when he opened his menu once more.

"The hamburgers?"

"Is that what you'd like? You can have anything."

"I like hamburgers."

He glanced at her over the top of his menu. "I'll have to remember that. Favorite food hamburgers."

"Wait a minute. I didn't say they were my favorite food. They are just one of the things I like to eat."

"Ah, well then, is there anything else you see that you might prefer?"

"*Nee*, not today. Today seems like a hamburger day."

"What other food do you like?" He placed the menu on the table. "I want to learn everything about you, Tulip."

"My favorite food is apple pie and ice cream, but only the pies that *Mamm* makes. I don't know what she does, but they taste better than anyone else's. What about you?" Tulip asked.

"What's my best and favorite?"

"*Jah.*"

"Roasted lamb, with the skin slightly crisp on the outside, along with baked vegetables and thick gravy."

Tulip giggled at the look on his face as he spoke about the food. "Stop. You're making me hungry. I love the crispy part too. The thing is that you mentioned more than one food. You just named quite a few. I only asked for one favorite food."

He leaned back. "Oh, sorry. I didn't know there were rules."

"There are. I said favorite food—as in one food."

"Strictly speaking, you can't call gravy a food, and it's just not the same to eat roasted lamb without the vegetables that go along with it. They're a group of foods. How's that?"

A waitress walked to the table to take their order.

"Would you like your hamburger with the lot, Tulip?" he asked.

Tulip closed her menu. *"Jah* please."

He looked up at the waitress. "That's two with the lot." Then he looked back at Tulip. "And what about to drink?"

"Just a soda, *denke.*"

After their order had been taken, they sat there looking at one another until they both laughed.

He reached out for her hand and held it in his. "I'm so pleased I came to the community and met you."

"Me too."

He glanced out the window. "It's getting dark. Did you tell your parents you might be late home? I don't fancy getting on the wrong side of them."

"I told them to expect me when they saw me."

"Good. That is good news. Now what else can you tell me about yourself?"

She looked at their clasped hands, not even the slightest bit concerned that someone might see them. Being affectionate with him seemed like a natural thing to do. "I can't reveal all about myself in one go. There'd be nothing to look forward to and nothing to learn later, would there?"

He chuckled. "I just want to know more … well, the truth is that I want to know everything about you."

"That wouldn't do. You have to be content with just a little bit for now."

"Really? It seems you have rules that I don't know about. You'll have to let me in on them."

Tulip laughed. "There are no rules, not really."

"Okay. That's good to know. I'm happy with what I

141

know about you so far. I'll have to be content with that for the time being."

They had to release each other's hands when the waitress brought their drinks to the table.

After they had a couple of mouthfuls of soda, their hamburgers arrived.

"That was fast," he said.

"It was and they look delicious."

When they finished eating, Tulip wanted to stay talking with him, but it wouldn't do to get home too late.

"Are you ready to go?" he asked.

Tulip nodded.

"Are you sure you don't want anything else?"

"I couldn't possibly fit another thing in."

He chuckled. "Neither could I and I very rarely say that."

When they walked out of the restaurant, he moved closer to her and held her hand.

"Denke for coming out with me tonight. I hope we have many more nights like these."

"Me too."

He helped her into the buggy, acting like a proper gentleman.

TULIP WALKED into her house after Wilhem had taken her home. Lily looked at her anxiously when she walked through the door.

"Oh, it's you," Lily said.

"Who were you expecting?" Tulip asked.

"Daisy, that's who! Nathanial was bringing her home after the singing and there's no sign of either of them."

"Do you mean Nathanial and Matthew are bringing Daisy home?"

"*Nee,* why don't you clean out your ears, Tulip? I'm here and Daisy isn't. Why would two men drive her home? That would be weird. Nathanial is bringing Daisy home. They like each other and don't pretend you didn't notice that when he was here for dinner."

"He doesn't like her!" Tulip blurted out before she could stop herself.

"What do you mean?"

"Forget it."

"*Nee,* tell me why you said that," Lily insisted.

"It's nothing." Tulip hurried to the kitchen and found her mother sitting down drinking a cup of tea.

"*Mamm,* did you know that Nathanial Schumacher is bringing Daisy home?"

"*Jah,* from the singing. Lily told me."

"*Mamm,* I said, *Nathanial Schumacher!*"

Lily had followed her into the kitchen. "What's wrong with you? You're saying that like he's a bad person or something. You're not the only one in the *haus* who can have a boyfriend."

Tulip ignored her sister and stared at her mother, looking for a different reaction.

"You were right, Tulip. Someone can't be judged by what their siblings have done. It's just not fair. Everyone is their own person," their mother said. "You told me yourself no one should hold him responsible for his *bruder's* actions."

"Maybe I was wrong!" Tulip said.

"You're jealous!" Lily said with a raised voice. "She doesn't want Daisy or me to have a boyfriend, *Mamm*. She thinks she's the only one who can have one. Tell her, *Mamm*."

"Hush, both of you."

"Both of us? I'm not raising my voice," Tulip said. "I'm just worried, that's all."

"Go up to your rooms. I'll be glad when you're all married and out of the *haus*. Go to your rooms now!"

Tulip left the room before Lily. She knew Lily was scowling at her, but didn't look her way. Why was she getting into trouble? She was only trying to warn her mother that Nathanial was trouble.

For the next few hours, Tulip paced up and down her bedroom worrying about Daisy. The girl was immature and Nathanial, well, he was deceitful at best. And what if he was like his brother in other ways? Tulip feared the worst, but didn't know what to do.

NANCY LEFT her husband reading the bible in the living room, waiting for Daisy to come home, while she went to bed. She felt bad for saying mean things to the girls just now, but sometimes they pushed her and tested her patience to the limit. One minute Tulip was defending Nathanial, and the next minute she was making out he wasn't to be trusted. Hezekiah thought Nathanial was a good man so she'd have to trust her husband's judgment.

Trusting her daughters with men was another thing

she was gradually trying to do as well. Each girl would have to rely on her own judgment at one point or another. She couldn't make every one of their decisions for them. Going on a buggy ride with a man might help Daisy mature a little. If one twin gained a little maturity it would surely influence the other. When Daisy came home, she would tell her not to be out so late in future.

After she took off her prayer *kapp* and brushed out her long hair, she changed into her nightgown. She'd kept out of Tulip's business as best she could in regard to Wilhem and things seemed to be working out well between them. She was there for Tulip to ask advice of and that seemed to be enough. Rose had needed a lot more guidance, but Tulip was the sensible one in the family out of all the girls.

Nancy walked to the window and looked out into the darkness. The warm glow of the moon lightened the darkness a little, and streetlights in the distance twinkled against the darkened landscape. There was no sign of a buggy bringing her daughter back home. It was then she saw a dark shadowy figure moving toward the house. She watched the figure come closer and saw a white prayer *kapp* and apron. The only girl who would be coming to the house this late at night would be Daisy. Why was she on foot?

"Hezekiah!" Nancy raced down the stairs and was met by Hezekiah's worried face. "It's Daisy coming to the house by herself!"

Hezekiah's eyes opened wide as though he couldn't believe his ears, and then he ran outside.

CHAPTER 22

Tulip heard her mother's screams and ran down the stairs right behind Lily.

As soon as she reached the bottom of the stairs, she saw her father bring Daisy into the house with his arm around her. She'd been crying, looked disheveled, and was out of breath, like she'd been running.

Their mother ran to Daisy and asked, "Where's Nathanial?"

"He tried to attack me. I ran away from him." Daisy sobbed into her father's shoulder and he encircled his arms around her.

Tulip and her mother gasped in shock.

"What?" their mother shrieked.

Lily ran to Daisy and hugged her. "He tried to attack you?"

Daisy nodded and then she rubbed her eyes.

"What happened?" their father asked, clearly trying to keep a level head.

"Didn't you hear her, *Dat?* He needs to be punished. Go punch him," Lily said.

Hezekiah shook his head. "It's not our way."

Lily curled her hands into fists. "So then—what? You can't let him get away with this."

"Are you hurt anywhere, Daisy?" their mother asked.

"Nee. I'm not. I should never have gone with him. You should've stopped me, *Mamm.* You'd never have let Rose go with someone you didn't know well. Don't you care about me as much as you care about Rose?"

Tulip looked at her mother and could see the hurt on her face at Daisy's words.

Tulip stepped in closer to Daisy. "You can't blame *Mamm.* Nathanial did this. He's the one to blame."

Their mother burst into tears. "It's all my fault. Daisy is right. I should never have let her go."

"Let's not find people to blame. Daisy, why don't you go into the kitchen with your *mudder* and have a cup of hot tea?"

Daisy wiped her eyes and nodded. "Okay."

He then said, "I'll talk to the bishop about this in the morning."

"Gut!" Lily yelled. "Finally, something will be done about him. I hope he's run out of town. I hate him! If I were a man, I'd go there right now and make him sorry he did what he did."

"That's not helping the matter, Lily," their father said quietly. "Now go help your *mudder* make the tea."

While the twins and their mother walked to the kitchen, Tulip stood by the bottom of the stairs, looking at her father. It couldn't have been easy not to head out the door and find Nathanial and have words with him. She could see by her father's face that he was dreadfully shaken. His whole face had turned a ghostly gray, almost a blue color.

"Are you okay, *Dat?*"

He nodded and then sat down in his chair, staring into the distance. She admired his self-control. Tulip was feeling the same outrage as Lily. They were both upset that a man would lay a hand on their sister and she could only imagine how their mother felt. If their father had raced out the door to confront Nathanial, she would've been scared for both of them. The Amish way was far better, as no good ever came from violence. The bishop would handle the whole thing and come up with some kind of resolution. In her heart, Tulip suspected that Nathanial would go back to Oakes County quite soon after everybody found out about this episode.

"*Dat*, would you like me to get you a cup of hot tea?"

"*Jah, denke,* Rose."

"It's Tulip, *Dat.*"

"Ah, sorry. *Denke,* Tulip."

Tulip walked into the kitchen to see Daisy dabbing at her eyes with a handkerchief.

"He tried to attack me, Tulip. I can't tell you more."

Tulip gasped. "That's just not right. Did you tell *Dat* anything else before you came inside the *haus?*"

She shook her head. "*Mamm* said she'll tell him again so that he can tell the bishop tomorrow."

"*Gut!*" Tulip put her arm around Daisy. "Don't you worry about anything. I'm sure he'll be leaving here soon."

"*Denke,* Tulip. I hope so."

When the pot boiled, Tulip made tea for everyone and then took a cup out to her father.

"Here's your tea, *Dat*." She looked closer to see that he had his eyes closed. It seemed odd that he had been so wide-awake and now he was sleeping after the huge drama that had just taken place. She touched him gently on his shoulder. "Dat." He didn't wake. Tulip touched him again and when he didn't respond she was suddenly certain he was dead. She dropped the tea and screamed. "*Mamm!*"

Everyone ran out from the kitchen.

"I think *Dat's* dead! He won't wake up."

Their mother rushed to feel for his pulse. "He's not dead! Quick, call 911!"

Tulip grabbed a lantern and the three girls headed to the barn.

NANCY STARED at her husband's lifeless-looking body. He was still breathing and had a pulse, but he wouldn't wake.

"I can't lose you, Hezekiah. We told each other we'd have more years alone when the girls get married. I need those years with you." Tears ran down her face. "Don't leave me alone. You can't." She sobbed. It had never occurred to her that she might lose her husband so soon before they reached old age.

The twins ran back inside. "They're coming. They're sending an ambulance. Tulip is still on the phone with them. They're asking her a lot of questions."

"What's wrong with him, *Mamm?*"

"I don't know, Daisy. I don't know."

CHAPTER 23

Twenty minutes later, Tulip stood with the twins at the front door, watching the ambulance leave with their father. Their mother had been allowed to travel to the hospital with him. They were told he might have fainted due to heart failure or possible hypertension.

"You know whose fault this is?" Lily said.

"It's Nathanial's fault. He gave *Dat* a heart attack. I could see by *Dat's* face something was wrong. He was filled with so much rage and he didn't let it out. I'm not going to let Nathanial get away with it," Tulip said.

"*Dat* said we shouldn't look for people to blame," Daisy said.

"*Dat's* not here! Lily, hand me that lantern." While Lily gave her the lantern, Tulip said, "Now come with me, both of you, and help me hitch the buggy."

"Where are we going?"

"We're not going anywhere. You're both staying here. I'm going to tell Nathanial what he did to our *vadder*."

"You can't go there. It's too late. You'll wake Mr. and Mrs. Schumacher," Daisy said.

"And Matthew," Lily added.

"Then they'll all hear what he's done." Tulip marched to the barn with a twin on each side. "As soon as I'm gone, call Rose, Trevor, and Peter—tell them about *Dat.*"

Tulip had ordered the twins to stay home, and given the mood she was in they obeyed.

BEFORE SHE KNEW IT, Tulip was right outside the Schumachers' front door.

Matthew stepped outside before she got out of the buggy. He walked forward and squinted at her in the dark. "Tulip, is that you?"

She jumped out of the buggy. "*Jah.* I'm here to see Nathanial."

"Okay, I'll get him."

Nathanial walked outside. "*Jah?* Why are you here so late, Tulip? If you've got anything to say to me, can't you do that at a reasonable hour?"

"You attacked my *schweschder.*"

Matthew stepped forward. "Is that true, Nathanial?"

"She's lying," Nathanial said out of the side of his mouth while he glared at Tulip.

"Not only did you assault Daisy, you caused my *vadder* to have a heart attack. He's in the hospital right now."

Matthew stepped forward. "Is he okay?"

"She's lying about everything. They're a *familye* of liars, Matthew."

"*Nee,* they aren't, Nathanial. I've known them all my

life and I've never known any of them to lie—not even once." He turned to Tulip. "Is there anything I can do?"

"*Nee*, Matthew. He's in the hospital. I hope he'll be all right. It's your fault, Nathanial."

Matthew stared at Nathanial, who turned away and walked back inside the house.

"Are you okay, Tulip? It must have given you all a dreadful fright. And Daisy, is she okay?"

"Daisy was really shaken over what he did to her. She ran away from him, and then she had to walk home all alone in the dark."

Matthew rubbed his chin. "*Mamm* and *Dat* won't want him to stay with us when they find out what's happened."

"I'm glad you came outside, Matthew. I wanted to hit him so badly just then when he denied what he did. *Dat* was going to tell the bishop about what he did in the morning. He won't be able to do that now. I'll have to go to the bishop and tell him myself."

"I know how you must feel. I'm sorry this whole thing has happened. I hope your *vadder* will be all right."

"Me too. I'll go home and call the hospital and see if they can tell me how he is."

"Do you want me to drive you home?"

"*Nee, denke*, Matthew. I'll need to cool down." Tulip was still mad, but felt better for telling Nathanial exactly how she felt. He wasn't a nice person at all. She was glad Matthew had been there to defend her from Nathanial's lies.

Tulip drove home in the darkness of night. She was very often scared of driving alone at night, but not this night. Sadness and anger mixed together held her fear at bay. The twins rushed out of the house as soon as she arrived home.

"What happened?" Daisy asked.

"Did you speak to Nathanial himself?" Lily asked.

Tulip jumped down from the buggy. "Before I tell you, did you ring Rose and the boys?"

"I did," Daisy said.

"Gut, denke."

"They were very worried. Trevor and Peter said they'd go to the hospital and Rose and Mark were going too."

"It makes me wish we could've gone too," Lily said.

"Nee, they might not have let you see him with them treating him and trying to find out what was wrong with him. It would've been a wasted trip. Best that we all stayed here."

"Did you see Nathanial and talk to him?" Daisy asked.

"Jah, Matthew came out of the house first and he brought Nathanial out and stayed in the background. He heard everything. Nathanial denied he did anything and walked inside as if he didn't even care. Matthew said his parents won't want him there after they hear what happened."

"So Matthew is going to tell his parents?" Daisy asked.

"Jah. Now help me unhitch the buggy." While the three of them worked to unhitch the buggy and rub down the horse, Tulip told them she would speak to the bishop herself tomorrow morning.

"Do you think you should wait until *Dat* is well enough to tell him?" Lily asked.

"We don't know how long he'll be in the hospital,"

Tulip said. "I'll call as soon as we're finished here and find out how he is."

"Will they tell you?" Daisy asked.

"I don't know but I'll try to find out."

"Don't worry about talking to the bishop tomorrow," Daisy said. "It's more important that *Dat's* okay."

"*Jah,* but I don't want to let Nathanial get away with it," Tulip said.

Lily wheeled the buggy into the barn while Daisy and Tulip rubbed down the horse.

When Lily came back, she said, "He won't get away with it, Tulip, but I think Daisy is right. We should forget about it until we know how *Dat* is and he's back home."

Daisy stopped what she was doing and covered her face with both hands. "It's all my fault. *Dat* might die and its all my fault for going on that stupid buggy ride with that horrible man." She sobbed uncontrollably and both her sisters rushed to her side and placed their arms around her.

"It's not your fault at all," Lily said. "Stop crying."

"Lily is right. It's not your fault and *Dat* would want us to be strong. I'll call the hospital now if you stop crying."

Daisy put her hands by her side while Lily wiped the tears away from Daisy's face.

Tulip called the hospital with a younger twin sister on either side. When she finally got through to someone, she was told he was currently being treated and was stable. Then she was asked to ring back in the morning. When she hung up the receiver, she told her sisters that he was okay and they wouldn't know any more until the morning.

"*Mamm* would say that the best thing we could do is get a good night's sleep," Lily said.

"That sounds like a good idea," Tulip said. "Let's get inside. It's getting cold out here."

When Tulip called the hospital early the next morning, she learned that her father had heart disease, but he was okay for now. He was awake and was due to be released that afternoon. She called her two brothers and then Rose and learned that they'd all come home from the hospital in the early hours of the morning. Tulip headed back to the house to let her sisters know the news.

"Is he going to die soon?" Daisy asked Tulip.

"I don't think so. They're giving him medication that he has to take daily, so I think he'll be okay for a few more years."

"I thought he was dead, or going to die," Lily said. "I didn't get a wink of sleep all night."

"Me too. I don't think any of us would've gotten any sleep, especially *Mamm*." Tulip thought back to the frightful moment when she couldn't wake her father and thought he had gone home to be with *Gott*. Until that moment, she'd never given any serious thought to losing either of her parents.

"Are you going to work today, Tulip?" Lily asked.

"I don't know. I had planned to go to the bishop. What do you think?"

"*Nee*. We talked about that last night and decided it's best that you don't," Daisy said. "Just wait until *Dat* is better and see what happens."

"Nathanial will probably leave of his own accord now that other people know what he's done," Lily said.

"*Jah,* I will go to work then. It sounds like *Dat* is not in any danger. You two can stay here and wait for *Mamm* and *Dat* to come home. See what you can fix for dinner."

"I hope Nathanial doesn't get away with everything that happened. Do you think he will?" Lily asked.

"Hopefully, he'll go away now after Tulip let Matthew know what happened." Daisy managed a laugh.

"I've never been so angry." Tulip placed a plate of eggs down on the table for the girls to help themselves. "It must've been a terrible fright for you, Daisy."

"It was. I jumped out of the buggy and ran away. At first I wasn't sure where I was, but then when I came to the corner I knew what street I was on. I was scared, too, because he kept yelling my name and I had to hide when he drove past looking for me."

TULIP WENT to work as usual. She didn't want to let Audrey down by calling in for a day off. She hoped that her father would be home by the time her shift was over.

When she finished work, she walked around the back of the shop to where the buggies were, and saw Wilhem waiting for her.

He stepped toward her. "Are you okay?"

She was pleased to see his friendly face. "You heard?"

"Everyone knows about Nathanial and about your *vadder* being in the hospital."

Tulip was glad everyone knew about Nathanial, but

hoped it wouldn't be twisted around to reflect badly on Daisy's reputation.

"How is your *vadder* doing now?"

"He has heart disease, and he fainted because not enough blood was getting to his brain. It gave us all a terrible fright. He should be okay now that he'll have medicine to take. The doctor told me that people live for many years with it. He's coming home this afternoon. He might even be home now."

"That's good news! And you might be happy to know that Nathanial is leaving town this afternoon."

Tulip heaved a sigh. "I'm so glad. That does make me happy."

"I heard you had a few words to say to him and woke up the Schumacher household."

"How did you hear about that?"

He laughed. "News travels."

"It certainly does."

"Is there anything I can do, Tulip, for you or your *familye?*"

She shook her head. *"Nee,* I don't think so, but *denke."*

"I just wanted to let you know that I'm thinking of you."

She smiled back at him. *"Denke.* That means a lot."

"I won't hold you up. You'll be anxious to see your *vadder."* He stepped away from her horse.

She climbed into the buggy. *"Denke.* It means a lot that you came here."

CHAPTER 24

On her drive home, Tulip wondered if Wilhem would be attracted to a girl who would wake up a household to yell at their visitor. One thing she knew for certain, her mother wouldn't be happy to find out about her outburst and since Wilhem had learned of it, her mother would be sure to find out.

Tulip was pleased to be able to give the twins the news that Nathanial had left. Now it wasn't so urgent that they speak to the bishop.

Not long after Tulip arrived home, Peter and Trevor and their wives, as well as Rose and Mark, drove up to the house to wait for their father to arrive home.

Tulip was the first of her sisters to hurry over and ask her sister-in-law if she could hold Shirley, her young niece. It was usually the twins who got there first to hold Shirley, but they were too upset about recent events to race their sister to their only niece.

When everyone was settled in the house, the twins were busy making tea when a taxi pulled up to the house.

Tulip's older brothers went outside to help their father inside.

"Don't give me any more frights," their father joked to everyone as he walked inside the house. "The old ticker won't be able to take it."

Peter glared at each of the twins. "What's this about giving *Dat* a fright?"

"Why do you assume it was one of us?" Lily asked.

"Hush," Rose said. *"Dat* doesn't need to hear squabbles."

"It's nothing to worry about," Tulip told Peter as she shifted Shirley from one hip to the other.

"Sit down, *Dat,"* Lily said.

"We'll look after you," Daisy said.

Peter helped *Dat* to the couch. Once he was seated, *Mamm* sat next to him.

"Tell us the news. What did the doctor say?" Trevor asked as everyone sat down in the living room.

"I'll let your *mudder* tell you." His voice was quiet, almost breathless.

They all looked expectantly at *Mamm.*

"He needs to take daily medication and if he does that he'll be okay. He'll live long enough to see all his *grosskinner* come into the world." She particularly looked at Amy and Trevor when she said that since they'd been married well over a year and they still had no children and weren't even expecting.

TULIP LEANED down and kissed her father on his cheek, and then she looked at her mother, who looked like she needed a good sleep. "How are you, *Mamm?"*

"I need a hot shower."

"Did you get any sleep at all?" Julie, one of her daughters-in-law, asked.

"*Nee,* I was sitting up all night worried about Hezekiah."

"I'm sorry to put you through that," he said.

"No need to be sorry."

Their father chuckled. "I'm all right."

"*Jah,* you are now. Now that they've given you heart medication," Daisy said.

"Just don't forget to take them," Lily added.

Dat opened his mouth to speak but *Mamm* got in first. "There's no chance of that with all of us here to remind him. He has to go back to the hospital every day for a while until they get the levels right," *Mamm* told them. "We don't want him passing out again."

"Are you going to faint or something again?" Daisy asked her father.

He pulled a face. "I hope not."

"He won't as long as he does everything the doctor said." *Mamm* stared at her husband.

His lips turned upward at the corners. "I will."

"You look really tired, *Dat,*" Rose said. "And very pale."

"That won't make him feel any better," Lily said to Rose.

"I feel a bit weak, that's all."

"Did you say you have to go to the hospital every day?" Tulip asked.

"*Jah,* then I'd reckon I'll have to be checked every few weeks for a bit, and then months."

"Don't talk so much. Just rest," *Mamm* said, putting a hand on her husband's shoulder.

"Tulip said that Nathanial has already left, *Dat*," Lily said as she moved to sit on the floor by her father's feet.

Tulip glanced at her father, worried about how he'd take the mention of Nathanial. The last thing he needed was to hear that name, and now Trevor and Peter would want to know what was happening in regard to Nathanial. They hadn't heard what had happened as yet.

"All things work together for good," he said.

"What's going on with Nathanial?" Peter asked.

Trevor added, "Who is Nathanial?"

"It's a story for another day, but not today," Tulip said.

When they heard a buggy, Daisy ran to the window, followed close behind by Lily who had leaped off the couch.

"It's Aunt Nerida and it looks like she's come by herself," Daisy said.

Tulip looked at her mother. *Mamm* and her younger sister had been having a feud for some time. The twins ran and opened the door while their mother stood still, looking exhausted.

A LITTLE PART of Nancy was pleased that her sister cared enough to visit even though she was still annoyed with her. Nerida must've heard about Hezekiah landing in the hospital. Nancy placed one foot in front of the other and reached the door just as Nerida stepped into the house.

"Nancy, I just heard the news. How is he?"

"He's better; he's home now."

Nerida looked over at Hezekiah on the couch. "You gave everyone a scare."

He chuckled and everyone greeted Nerida and then there was silence in the room as the two women stood face-to-face, staring at each other. "Are you okay, Nancy?"

"As good as I can be. A night in the chair at the hospital has taken its toll."

"You need to rest, Nancy," Hezekiah called from the couch.

"Don't you worry about me, Hezekiah. You just worry about yourself."

Everyone laughed.

"*Denke* for coming, Nerida," Nancy said. Being with her sister gave her a sense of comfort and reminded her of days gone by.

"Of course I'd come. I came as soon as I heard. You should've called me."

"Would you like to stay for dinner?" Tulip asked her aunt.

Before Nerida could answer, Nancy said to Tulip, "Have you arranged dinner?"

Tulip said, "*Jah*. Everyone can stay for dinner. The twins fixed something, and there's plenty for all of us."

Everyone accepted the dinner invitation except for Nerida.

"Maybe another time," Nerida said. "I've left the girls at home alone. They wanted to come, but I told them I wouldn't be long. Now that I know you're okay, Hezekiah, I better get back to the girls and to John." Nerida turned and walked away, stepping out the door.

"*Denke* for coming," Nancy called after her younger sister.

"Of course I would come," came the reply.

It had been a while since Nancy had all her children in the home and, although she was pleased to have them there, the circumstances could've been better.

"It was very nice of Aunt Nerida, coming to see how *Dat* was, wasn't it *Mamm?*"

"Mmm. Now if you'll all excuse me, I need a shower. You girls see what you can do about getting dinner served and the table set."

"*Jah Mamm*," the twins chorused.

Nancy walked up the stairs, relieved that Hezekiah was going to be okay. He was always the one who'd told her to enjoy the day they were living right now rather than think they'd enjoy some future day in a future time. Nancy knew she had a habit of looking forward to the future, and particularly to the time when Hezekiah and she could be alone once more. It was a lesson learned now that she'd nearly lost him. Now she'd enjoy each day she got to spend with him.

As THE BEADS of hot water pelted over Nancy's body, all of the tension left her. She hadn't realized how tightly she'd been holding her body until she'd told herself to relax. Tonight, she'd enjoy having the whole family gathered around the table and under the one roof.

She would talk to her entire family and insist that they all have dinner at the house once a month. After the scare with Hezekiah, she intended to make the most of each and every day with her family. One day, things might mend between her sister and herself. Nerida had made a step, which had given Nancy hope. Now it was up to her to make the next step. If only Nerida had apologized years ago then things wouldn't have gotten this far. Maybe she had to let the whole thing slide rather than wait for an apology that she was clearly never going to get.

Nancy decided to put the step she'd make toward Nerida out of her mind for the moment. What was important right now was enjoying her entire family and thanking God that they were all together.

CHAPTER 25

The doctor at the hospital was pleased with Hezekiah's progress over the next few days and now they were satisfied that he was on the correct level of medication.

When Nancy went downstairs on Saturday morning, Tulip and the twins were already at the kitchen table, talking.

Tulip looked up at *Mamm* when she entered the room. "Can we all go today and choose some material for new dresses? We haven't had any for some time. I have enough money to pay for all of the material for the three of us."

"That's not necessary, Tulip," *Mamm* said, pleased by the sudden generosity.

"I don't mind. I've nothing else to spend my money on."

"I'm okay with her spending her money on me," Lily said with a giggle.

"Me too," Daisy added. "I'll pay you back when I get a job, Tulip."

Lily scowled at her twin. "You'll never get a job. You're not even looking for one."

"I've been thinking about it."

"You never told me you even wanted one."

"Quiet, girls. You can go into town by yourselves. I'm not feeling too well today, but the three of you can go if that's what you want. At least I might have some quiet around here while you're gone."

"We won't go if you're sick," Tulip said.

"I'll stay with *Mamm* if you and Lily want to get the material," Daisy said. "Just get me dark colored fabric. Maybe purple or something nice."

"*Denke* Daisy, but we can wait until *Mamm's* better so that all four of us can go together."

"You might as well go today. I can see how excited you are. The sooner you get the material, the sooner we can get started on sewing the dresses."

"Are you sure, *Mamm?*" Tulip asked.

"*Jah,* you and Lily can choose it and Daisy and I will stay here."

"Yeah, I don't mind at all," Daisy said, putting her arm around her mother. "I'll look after *Mamm.*"

Hezekiah was still in bed. It would be a long time before he'd be able to go back to work helping his brother on his farm—if ever. The girls made Nancy sit down on the couch while they made her breakfast.

It was rare that the twins did things separately and Nancy was glad to have the chance to speak to Daisy alone. They hadn't talked since Daisy had gone through the awful experience with Nathanial, and Nancy hoped that the scare she'd had wasn't going to affect her finding a husband. It was important for Daisy to know that what had happened to her was a very rare thing to happen in their community and totally not something that should be accepted. As soon as Hezekiah gained strength he'd let the bishop know what had happened and then Nathanial's bishop would certainly be informed of the event.

When Lily and Tulip headed off in the buggy after breakfast, Daisy sat down next to her mother. "Can I get you anything, *Mamm?* Some more tea?"

"*Nee,* I'm fine. I'm glad you stayed here with me. We haven't had much of a chance to talk lately."

"Is there something on your mind that you want to say?" Daisy asked.

"I hoped we might have a conversation about what happened with Nathanial."

Daisy scowled. "I don't want to talk about that. Anyway, I already told you what happened that night."

"Well, not really. What you said was quite vague and then he left so no one heard his side."

"What do you mean by 'his side?'" Daisy sprang to her feet. "Don't you believe me?"

Nancy closed her eyes for a moment. She was too tired for this. "Sit down! Of course I believe you. I just want to talk about it. I am your *mudder,* so you should be able to talk with me about everything, *jah?*"

Daisy obeyed her mother and sat back down. "Except that. I don't want to talk about him and how horrible he is. It just brings back awful memories. He's gone now anyway and I'm glad. He's back where he belongs, back where he came from, and far away from me."

Nancy stared at her daughter and she was sure that

Daisy was keeping something from her, but now was not the time to find out what it was. She'd find out soon enough because she always managed to find out the secrets that her children kept from her.

Nancy's mind drifted back to her estranged sister. Her coming there to see how Hezekiah was showed her that they'd always be there for one another when it counted. Even when they didn't like each other, their bond as sisters would never be broken. Being the younger two in the family, and the only girls, they'd been so close years ago. It didn't feel right with her not being around. The feud had lasted years, each waiting for the other to be the first to make amends. Nancy sighed deeply.

She had to do something to show Nerida that she wanted her back in her life. That most likely meant she would have to forego that apology and that was something that didn't sit well with her.

"Is everything okay, *Mamm?*"

"*Jah,* it is."

"You look like you're worried about something. If it's me you're worried about, you don't need to be. Everything is perfectly fine. Nathanial has gone so everything is okay."

Nancy was slightly amused at her daughter's words. It was typical of her to think that everything was about her.

"That's better. You're smiling now."

"Maybe I'll have that hot tea now *denke,* Daisy."

"Sure, coming up." She leaned over and gave her mother a kiss on the cheek.

When Tulip and Lily had finished selecting the fabric for the new dresses, Lily suggested, "Why don't we visit Rose now?"

"At the markets?"

"*Jah.* She'd be working today, wouldn't she?"

"I think so. That's a good idea. We're not that far away. We can leave this parcel in the buggy so we don't lose it somewhere."

The girls stopped at their buggy and then continued to the farmers market where Rose worked at the flower stall. It was lunchtime when they arrived there and they walked through until they saw Rose's stall.

"She's got customers," Lily said.

"We'll just wait nearby to speak with her in between customers."

While they waited, they caught sight of Matthew Schumacher who was working at the stall next to Rose.

Seeing he had no customers, he walked the six strides over to them to say hello. "Hi, Tulip, and Lily."

Lily frowned at him. "How do you know I'm Lily?"

Tulip hadn't picked up on that, but now that Lily had mentioned it, Tulip found it odd. No one had ever been able to pick the identical twins apart—no one outside of the family, that was.

Matthew chuckled. "I know you're Lily because Daisy just looks different."

Lily pouted. "How so?"

Tulip noticed, by Matthew shifting his weight uncomfortably from one foot to the other, that he was uncomfortable with the question.

"Just different."

"We look the same. Many people say exactly the same and no one but our family can tell us apart. How can you tell us apart?"

"Well, Daisy has got three tiny freckles on each cheek. They're like small pinpoints and to me, her eyebrows look a little darker."

Lily frowned and stared at Tulip. "That's quite unbelievable. She does have those freckles."

"I know." Matthew excused himself when people walked up to his stall.

"What do you think about that, Tulip?" Lily asked in amazement.

"Weird."

"He's in love with Daisy."

Tulip couldn't resist saying, "How do you know he's not in love with you?"

"Do you think so?" Lily stared back at Matthew. "I've never thought of him in that way, but he doesn't have a twin and Daisy and I always said we would marry twins."

"It looks like Matthew misses out on both of you, then." Seeing Rose was now free, Tulip held onto Lily's arm and they both walked forward to say hello.

"So sorry. I've been busy like this all day."

"We came into town to get some material to make dresses," Lily said.

"Did you get any?" Rose asked.

"Oh, Tulip, we should've brought it with us to show Rose."

"*Jah*, I didn't even think of that."

Rose looked around. "Where's Daisy?"

"Home with *Mamm*. She didn't feel too good so Daisy said she would stay home with her."

"I think she's just tired," Tulip added so Rose wouldn't worry. It was bad enough worrying about one parent.

"And you've got the day off, Tulip?"

"Jah, a rare day off. I'm enjoying it."

"Can you come and have lunch with us, Rose?" Lily asked.

"Nee, she can't leave the stall. She brings food, and so do I when I work here."

"Boring!"

Rose and Tulip laughed.

"Can we bring you back something to eat, or a cup of coffee?" Lily asked.

"I'm fine, *denke."*

"Okay."

Tulip noticed Lily give Matthew a sidelong glance.

"I guess we should keep going, Lily."

"We're going to have lunch somewhere, aren't we?"

"Jah, okay. We'll have lunch then we'll go home and sew."

They said goodbye to Rose and waved to Matthew, who was still serving customers. Just outside the markets, they found a café where they had lunch. All the while Tulip was doing her best to stop thinking about Wilhem, wondering where he was and what he was doing.

THE NEXT TIME Tulip saw Wilhem was Monday morning at the cake shop. He'd walked in, and now he was standing in front of her.

"Are you here to see me?" she asked. She had hoped to see him over the weekend. He'd certainly been on her mind every moment of the last couple of days.

"I'm here for a cup of coffee and to see you."

"You could've mentioned me first, before the coffee, at least."

He smiled and walked closer to her. A glass display cabinet that formed the counter stood between them.

"What will you have?" she asked.

"Just a black coffee today."

"Okay." She walked over and stood in front of the steel coffee machine, shook out a measure of freshly-ground coffee beans, and pressed it into the round container.

"How is your *vadder* today?" he asked.

"He's doing well. They say he'll be all right. He gave everyone a real scare."

"I can imagine he did."

After she pressed the button for the boiling water, she looked over the top of the machine. "How are you settling into the new *haus?*"

"It's great and I'm glad you brought that up. That's why I'm here. I wanted to ask you—"

"For decorating advice?" Tulip gave a little giggle at her own joke.

He laughed. "*Nee,* although some advice probably wouldn't go astray. We've gone for the functional look rather than the ..." He laughed. "I can't think of any other look."

Tulip was pleased that he was the only customer in the shop and the rest of the staff were working in the back.

"Tulip, have dinner with me tonight at my place?"

"I'd like that."

"Good. Shall we say, around seven? I'll come and collect you."

"*Nee*, I'll drive myself."

"Are you sure you want to do that?"

"*Jah.* Otherwise, you've got too much driving to do, back and forward, back and forward."

"I don't mind."

"*Nee*, it's okay. I'll drive myself. Would you like me to bring anything?"

He smiled again. "Just yourself."

Tulip took the filled-to-the-brim take-out cup and fitted a lid onto it. When she handed it to him, his fingertips brushed across hers. She withdrew her hand as a tingle rippled through her body. Had he done that on purpose?

He smiled as though he had. "I'll see you tonight, Tulip."

She nodded and then watched him turn and walk out of the shop. When her eyes dropped to the counter, she saw that at some point he'd placed the money there to pay for the coffee. Tulip giggled to herself. She'd been so distracted by him, she hadn't thought to ask for the money. It reminded her of their very first encounter, when she'd forgotten to pay at the café. Tulip placed the coins in the till and went into the back room to help the girls make tickets for the new cake varieties that Audrey was introducing.

. . .

After work, Tulip walked into her house. Her father was sitting on the couch.

"Hi, *Dat.*"

"Hello, Tulip. How was your day?"

"Good. The same as most days. I can't complain."

"That's good."

"Will it be all right with you if I go to Wilhem's house for dinner tonight? I won't be home late."

"Who will be there?" he asked.

"Where do you want to go?" Her mother came out of the kitchen wiping her hands on a hand towel.

"I was just asking *Dat* if it is all right if I go to Wilhem's *haus* for dinner tonight?"

"Who else will be there?" she asked.

"No one. It'll just be the two of us. At least, I think it will be the two of us. He didn't mention that Jonathan would be there. Is that all right?"

She watched her mother and father exchange looks before her mother said, "That's fine, but don't be late home. And we're trusting you."

"Of course."

"Your *vadder* doesn't need any more surprises."

"None of us do," Tulip said.

"I must have known you were going out somewhere because I've just baked two batches of whoopie pies. You can take some with you."

"That's not necessary *denke, Mamm.*"

"You can't show up there empty-handed. It's rude." She

looked her daughter up and down. "You go and clean yourself up and I'll find a basket for the whoopie pies."

"Denke." Tulip headed to the shower before her parents changed their minds. They both liked Wilhem, that was clear, or they wouldn't have let her go to his house for dinner.

JUST AS TULIP approached Wilhem's place, she noticed smoke coming out of the half opened windows. There wasn't enough smoke for the house to be on fire; it seemed to Tulip that someone might have lit a fire in the fireplace and the chimney was blocked or needed cleaning.

After she got out of the buggy, she tied her horse to the post and walked in the already open door. "Hello?" she called out.

Wilhem appeared, coming out from the kitchen with a white tea towel in his hand and looking flustered.

"What's going on?" she asked.

"I burned the dinner."

"What?"

"I burned the dinner."

"I heard you. I'm just surprised that you could do that."

He shook his head. "I planned a nice dinner and now it's ruined."

"I thought the smoke was coming from the fireplace. Is all this smoke coming from what's left of our dinner?"

"I'm afraid so, and now we have nothing to eat. Unless you'd like some stale bread? Or we could get take-out?"

Tulip giggled. "We do have whoopie pies thanks to my *mudder*."

"We do?" His face brightened.

"She insisted I bring them. I'll get them out of the buggy." After she pulled the basket of pies out of the buggy, she moved back the lid of the basket and showed him the pies.

"That'll do me. Would it be bad if we had dessert and nothing else?"

"I wouldn't mind. I've always wanted to do that. Surely it wouldn't hurt us to do that just the once."

"Okay. I'm game." He looked back at the house. "It's too smoky to go inside. We could eat on the porch."

"That'll be fine as long as the fire's out and everything."

"No cause for alarm—literally—and no need for the fire department."

"I'm happy to hear it. As long as everything is under control."

"You sit down." He took the basket from her and then disappeared inside while she sat on one of the two chairs on the porch. Moments later, he returned with two blankets and the whoopie pies on a plate.

He placed the pies down on the table between the two chairs and then spread a blanket over her knees.

"Great, *denke*. It's a bit chilly."

Once he was seated, he pulled his blanket over his lap and leaned closer to her. "I'll make this up to you. I owe you a proper cooked dinner. As soon as I learn how to cook properly, that's what you'll get."

She giggled and picked up a whoopie pie. "Instead of

waiting for something that'll never happen, why don't you come for dinner one night at my *haus?*"

"With your *familye?*"

"*Jah,* why not?"

"Yeah, I'd like that."

She took a bite of pie and when she'd swallowed her mouthful, she said, "I'm glad my *mudder* forced me to bring these."

"'Mother knows best'—isn't that what they say?"

"I haven't heard that, but maybe they do." She munched on her whoopie pie and then wondered where Jonathon was. "Where's your housemate tonight?"

Wilhem's brown eyes widened. "He's out with a girl."

"Really?"

He nodded with a hint of a smirk touching his lips.

"Who?"

He chuckled and shook his head at her. "You can't ask me things like that."

"It doesn't matter. I know who it is."

"Do you?"

"*Jah,* I do. It's obvious. How are you going to get all that smoke out of the *haus?*"

"I've opened all the doors and windows and with this breeze, I'm hoping all the smoke will be blown out."

"Everything will probably smell like smoke for a while."

He took a bite of pie and they ate in silence for the next few moments. "There's something I want to say to you, Tulip."

She frowned at him. "Good or bad?"

"Good—I think. Well, it's possibly good." He looked

out across the fields and then back to her. "I don't want there to be any misunderstanding between the two of us. I would like it very much if you and I only saw each other and no one else."

"You mean like boyfriend and girlfriend?"

"Exactly like that."

"I would like that, too."

"You would?" When she nodded, he made a motion like wiping sweat off his forehead, causing her to giggle at him. "Phew. I was hoping you would agree. I thought you might have felt the same way as I do, but I didn't want there to be any misunderstanding just in case."

"I'm glad you said that; it's easy to have misunderstandings." Tulip was so happy she felt she would burst. Although it was too cold to be sitting outside and the dinner had been burned, it truly was the company that made the difference—nothing else mattered. "I do have to tell you that a long time ago Nathanial kind of made out to me that you had to leave your old community, or something. I think he was hinting to me that you had a girlfriend."

"He would've been saying that because he wanted you for himself mostly, but there was an element of truth in what he said."

Tulip stared at him, waiting for him to continue.

"I was nearly married to a girl and then changed my mind a few weeks before we married." He looked sad as his gaze fell to the boards of the porch underneath their feet. "It was a terrible thing to do and I felt really bad about it, but I just couldn't go through with it."

Although it wasn't the worst news Tulip could've

heard, she still wasn't happy about it. Was he a man who didn't know his own mind? Shouldn't he have been sure about the girl before he asked for her to marry him?

He looked up at her. "Say something."

"Oh, I'm just a bit surprised, that's all."

"Does it make you think any less of me?"

"Not really, but it does give me some questions." Tulip answered as honestly as she possibly could.

"Tell me what questions you have and I'll do my best to answer them for you."

At that moment, all Tulip wanted to do was go home. She thought she'd found the perfect man and everything would work out perfectly and now she just wanted to be back in the safety of her house with her family. She sprang to her feet. "Can we talk about this another time? So much has happened with *Dat* being sick and what happened the other night with Daisy."

He stood up as well. "It does bother you."

"I don't really know. I just need some time to think about things." She took a couple of steps back.

"Don't go, Tulip. We can talk about this. Adele wasn't the right woman for me and I knew that."

Adele? Maybe she was being silly, but the fact that he had nearly married a woman called Adele that she didn't even know made Wilhem feel like a total stranger. Wilhem had been her picture of a perfect man and now she didn't know who he was. In her mind's eye, she saw a young woman called Adele crying over him and here he was in a different community asking another girl to be his girlfriend after he'd just broken Adele's heart. It didn't feel right.

Tulip looked at his pleading eyes and opened her mouth to speak but no words came out. She turned and walked to her buggy.

"Where are you going?" He followed after her.

"Home."

"Why has this upset you so much?" he asked.

She couldn't articulate why this felt wrong to her; there were so many reasons why it did. "I don't know, Wilhem. I don't think we should see each other for a while."

His mouth fell open in shock. "Is that what you really want? Because that's not what you said a moment ago."

"I didn't know that you are capable of breaking a woman's heart a moment ago."

He stepped closer to her. "Break ups aren't easy on anyone. It was better to happen before we got married than for us to go ahead with the wedding and have a miserable marriage. Don't you think so?"

"If you didn't get along, why did you ask her to marry you?" Tulip shook her head. "Don't answer that."

"I've got nothing to hide. I want to tell you everything."

Tulip had had too much drama over the past weeks, enough to last her for some time. As well as that, the horrible incidents that she'd had with Nathanial were still fresh in her mind. "Can we talk about this later? I need to go." She climbed up into the buggy and took hold of the leather reins.

He stepped closer to her. "We kind of fell into things because our parents wanted us to marry. I went along with it all without thinking too much about it, and then when I spent more time with her I realized we were totally unsuitable. By that time, I didn't have the courage to end things. That's why I left it so long."

Now he'd caught her attention. "What do you mean by the courage to end things?" To her, ending something seemed cowardly.

"It was a hard thing to do. I knew Adele would be upset, and all her friends and family, after they'd been planning the wedding. I had it in my mind I would just go along with it, but in the end I just couldn't go through with it. Everyone was mad with me and I knew they would be. I knew everybody was staring at me and talking about me, so I just had to get away for a while and that's why I came here. My parents weren't happy with me either because I'd gone back on my word. To me, it would have been worse to go ahead when I wasn't in love."

Tulip looked down at her hands and saw that she had been holding onto the reins so tightly that her knuckles had gone white.

"You see, Tulip, I was caught in a trap and there was no way out where everyone would be happy. If I'd gone ahead and married her, things would've been bad, and if I didn't, they would've been bad too. In the end, Adele deserved to be with a man who truly loved her and that man wasn't me." He shook his head.

She appreciated the way he was so calm and explained things to her so nicely. *"Denke* for telling me all that."

"So, do you feel better about the whole thing now that I've told you how it was?"

"I do."

A slight frown marred his perfect forehead. "Are you going to get down from that buggy?"

"I really should get home to my parents. Things haven't been easy for them lately."

"I understand, but are things between us okay?"

Tulip nodded. "They are. I'm just not good with surprises and I tend to think the worst."

"*Denke* for coming here tonight. You will go out with me again, won't you?"

"Of course I will."

"*Gut.* I might see you at work tomorrow when I call in for coffee. And I'm sorry again about dinner."

Tulip managed a little laugh. "You should try and get the smoke smell out of the house before Jonathan comes home."

Wilhem grinned. "*Jah,* I'll do that right now." He took hold of the horse's cheek strap and turned him toward the road. "Bye, Tulip," he said as he stopped and let go of the horse. The horse walked past him.

"I'll see you later." Tulip needed to process everything. It was a huge shock to learn that he'd gone back on his word. She'd always seen herself with someone who was upstanding and true to his word. It seemed like Wilhem wasn't the man she hoped he was. More than anything, Tulip wanted to marry a good man like her father. What she needed was to tell Rose what happened and listen to her opinion about the matter. She hoped Rose wouldn't mind her stopping by unexpectedly at this hour of the evening.

When she stopped her horse and buggy outside Rose and Mark's *haus,* Mark came outside to meet her.

"Oh, it's you, Tulip. I couldn't see who it was in the dark. Is your *vadder* okay?"

"*Jah,* he's fine. I wanted to steal your new *fraa* away for a couple of moments if that's okay. I need some older *schweschder* advice."

"Sure. She's in the kitchen. We've just finished dinner. You head inside and I'll secure your horse and give him some water."

"*Denke,* Mark."

"Hello," Tulip called out as she stepped through the doorway into Rose's house.

Rose came to the doorway of the kitchen and then went to hug her. "What are you doing here? Is everything okay?"

"*Dat's* fine if that's what you mean."

"What's going on? Why are you here so late? Not that I'm complaining. It's nice to have you here at whatever time of the day, or night."

"Can we sit down? I need to ask your advice about something."

"Come into the kitchen."

When they were both seated, Tulip began, "Wilhem invited me to dinner at his *haus* that he shares with Jonathon. He made a mess of things because the dinner got burned because he can't cook, and anyway, we ended up sitting out on the porch and then he told me something that shocked me. And if I hadn't brought it up, I might never have known."

"How could you have brought it up if you didn't know about it?"

"Nathanial hinted at something not been right with Wilhem and the reason he was here." She leaned in and whispered, "He hinted it was something like the reason that Jacob had come here."

"What did you find out?" Rose asked, leaning forward slightly.

"I don't know if I'm overreacting, and I need your advice. It wasn't as bad as the Jacob situation. I shouldn't have brought that up." Tulip took a deep breath. "Wilhem was supposed to be marrying someone and he ended the relationship just weeks before the wedding. He said their parents expected them to get married and he was just going along with it. Then he decided that they didn't really get along enough to be married."

"What's wrong with that?" Rose asked. "Is the girl—"

"Nee, nothing like that. I just keep picturing the poor girl being so upset that he ended things. He said she deserved to be married to someone who loved her."

"I can't see what the problem is. It's not as though he got married."

"I know, but I just wanted someone fresh, with no past. It was a shock for me to find that out. I wouldn't mind someone to have had a girlfriend or even two or three, but to have actually arranged a whole wedding and everything—"

"If he told you so soon, it doesn't sound like he was deliberately keeping it from you."

Tulip sighed. "Before he told me, he said he wanted me to be his girlfriend."

"That's *wunderbaar.* That's what you want, isn't it?"

"That's what I wanted. It's just that with all the drama you went through with Jacob and then all the fuss with

Nathanial, I just want someone with no bad things in their past."

"He didn't want to marry the girl and he was honest. You can't blame him for that."

"I know that, but it sounded like he wasn't honest about it for a long time and he should've ended things sooner if that was the case." Tulip rubbed her forehead, hoping she was explaining her feelings properly to Rose.

"People learn from their mistakes. He was young at the time and probably thought he was doing the right thing going along with what his parents wanted, until he thought about the rest of his life with the woman he didn't love."

"I know, but did he love her and then change his mind? That's what I'm really worried about. I don't want to be with someone changeable like that."

"You have to ask him that."

Tulip slowly nodded. *"Denke* for talking to me. I feel a little better about things now."

"How's everyone at home?"

"Good. It feels a bit strange there without you."

"Come over here any time. You can even stay for a few days if you want to."

Tulip giggled. "You're newlyweds. I wouldn't want to get in the way."

"Do you want some hot tea or something to eat, perhaps?"

Right on cue, Tulip's stomach growled, possibly objecting to the whoopie pies that she'd eaten instead of a proper dinner. Tulip laughed. "Did you hear that?"

"Was that your stomach?"

"*Jah.* I wouldn't mind something to eat, *denke.*"

"I can make you a sandwich with the leftover meat from dinner."

"Sounds delicious."

"We only had meatloaf."

"I love meatloaf."

Rose giggled and pulled out the leftovers from the gas-powered fridge. "You can give me a hand by slicing the bread."

Tulip stood up and opened the bread bin and pulled out the nearly full loaf. As she sawed through the bread with the serrated knife, her thoughts turned back to what Wilhem had told her. "Tell me honestly, Rose, do you think I'm worrying too much about nothing?"

"It sounds like you might be." She put a hand out for the bread and when Tulip handed her the two slices, she asked, "Butter?"

"*Nee denke.* It's fine like that."

"There you are." Rose handed her the sandwich on a plate and they both sat back down.

"I'm really hungry and this looks so good." She bit into the sandwich.

"I think you just worry because we've both had troubling things happen to us. Me with Jacob and you with Nathanial, and then there was what happened to Daisy with Nathanial. Wilhem's nothing like them from what I know of him and from what you've told me about him."

Tulip finished chewing. "I believe what he said, but it just doesn't feel perfect anymore."

"But maybe it is perfect and you should appreciate that rather than worrying about how you thought things should be or would be. He obviously really likes you a lot, so don't let what happened in the past come between the two of you. Besides, it wasn't his fault that his parents wanted him to marry that girl—the wrong girl. None of it was really his doing from what you told me."

"He shouldn't have let himself get dragged into it." Tulip looked down at the second-hand wooden kitchen table, scratched and marked from years of wear. Rose and Mark didn't have much to start their married lives, but they were happy. All they needed was each other. Mark was an honest man and she wanted someone like that. He'd only ever loved Rose. There had never been another woman in his life.

"I told you before, these things come with maturity and he was probably trying to please his parents and that's got to be a good thing." Rose leaned in closer, and whispered, "I always thought I would marry a man a lot taller than me and who looked different from Mark. There was this picture in my mind, and that picture became Jacob when I saw him."

"That was a total disaster."

"It was, and my perfect man was there all along right in front of me and I didn't know it. Maybe if Jacob hadn't jolted me out of my silliness, or whatever it was, my eyes would never have opened to see Mark." Rose tapped on the side of her head with her finger. "It's the ideas we've stored in our head about how our husbands should be that ruin things for us."

"I suppose that's true."

"It is and just like I always thought my husband would look a certain way, it sounds to me that you wanted someone who had never had an upheaval with a woman in his past. I just don't think that's realistic if you want someone older than yourself. Most boys start going out with girls at sixteen or seventeen. If you find someone special, you have to hold onto them, overlook the small things, and be grateful that they have the qualities that are important."

Tulip exhaled deeply. "I know you're right, but it's not knowing all the details of when he was about to get married that worries me. Just think, if he and I get married, he would've gone through all the pre-wedding stuff before. It's kind of ruined."

"You should be pleased that he didn't get married. If he had, you would never have met him."

"I know, I know. I thought about that."

"Do you think he's lying to you about something or not telling you the whole truth?"

"*Nee.*"

"Then what are you worried about? Just ask him anything you want to know."

Tulip finished off the last portion of her sandwich while thinking about all that her older sister had just said.

Rose continued, "You're probably just upset about what happened to *Dat* with his heart problem. That's upset everybody."

"It gave me a real scare. I thought he was dead there for a moment. You're right. I don't think I've gotten over that shock." Tulip dusted the crumbs from her hands. "*Denke* again for the sandwich. I should go now. I'm glad we talked."

"Me too."

The sisters hugged before Tulip walked with her sister to the front door. "Bye, Mark," she said when she saw him reading the paper on the couch. *"Denke* for taking care of the horse and letting me have ten minutes with Rose."

He chuckled. "Any time. Bye, Tulip. It was good to see you again."

"Bye." Tulip stepped out into the cold night air.

During the short ride back to her house, she decided to put Wilhem out of her mind for a day or two. Then she might be able to see things a little clearer. She was certain Rose was right, and she had to wait until she got used to the idea that things weren't as she thought they were. What probably annoyed her most was that Nathanial had hinted that Wilhem was there to get away from a problem and it turned out that he was right.

When Tulip walked into the house, instead of her mother and father on the couch, there were Daisy and Lily. "Have *Mamm* and *Dat* gone to bed already?"

"Jah. How was your big date night?" Lily asked.

Tulip put on a bright smile, not wanting the twins to know that she was upset. "It was a lot of fun." She sat down on the couch with them.

"What did you do?" asked Daisy.

"Just this and that. He cooked dinner for me but then burned it. What did you two do tonight?"

Daisy nodded her head at some sewing on a table nearby. "We finished off some of our sewing that we started the other day."

"Jah, and then we got tired of doing that."

"And we were just about to go to bed when we heard

the buggy outside, so we thought we'd wait up to hear about your night."

"Can you give us a few details about what happened on your date?" Daisy asked.

"Did you kiss him?" Lily asked, which made Daisy giggle.

"I can't tell you about things like that. *Nee,* I didn't, if you must know. Anyway, what about the two of you? I saw you both talking to men at Rose's wedding. Do either of you like anyone?"

"Why would we tell you if we did?" Lily asked.

"Because I just told you an answer to the question you asked me. That's why."

"Jah, Lily, tell her who you're interested in," Daisy said.

"Me? Why don't you tell her who you're interested in?"

Tulip giggled. As annoying as the twins were, she was glad to be home among everything that was familiar. When she was at home, she didn't have to worry about stepping out of her comfort zone. Maybe she wasn't ready for a real boyfriend just yet, even though many of the people her age in the community were now married. Perhaps she was just a late bloomer.

"What's funny?" Daisy asked, staring into Tulip's face.

"Life's funny in many ways."

Lily rolled her eyes. "You won't get any sense out of her because she's in love."

"Then why didn't you kiss him?" Daisy asked.

"I don't know him well enough."

When Tulip saw Daisy and Lily exchange glances, she explained, "I'm not going to kiss anyone until I know them really well, until I'm in love."

"See, Lily, she's not in love yet."

"I think she is because she keeps smiling. Unless she's not telling us the truth. Are you lying to us, Tulip?"

"I'd have absolutely no reason to do that."

"Why are you grinning like you've got a secret then?" Lily asked.

Tulip replied, "I didn't know I was."

"This is boring. I'm going to bed." Daisy jumped to her feet.

"Wait up." Lily stood as well and then they took a lamp upstairs with them, leaving Tulip alone.

Tulip leaned back on the couch with her hands behind her head. It wasn't often she could sit down in the peace and quiet. The house was always so noisy. To keep her mind off the man she was trying not to think about, she leaned forward and picked up one of the twins' sewing and began where she had left off.

THE NEXT TIME Tulip saw Wilhem was two days later when she was leaving work. She was pleased to see him leaning against her buggy.

He straightened up when he saw her approach. "Hello. I hope it's all right, me being here."

"It is."

"Things were kind of left a bit awkward the other night when I burned the food."

A small giggle escaped Tulip's lips when she thought about the smoke-filled house. He leaned down beside him and picked up a basket. "You left this basket at my *haus.*"

"You didn't have to make a special trip. We've got plenty of baskets."

"I wanted to see you." He took a step closer. "I know you were upset the other night to learn about Adele, but there's no reason to be."

"I'm just upset for her, that's all. She must've been very disappointed."

"She might've been more disappointed if we had married and the feelings weren't there between us."

"Wilhem, the thing that I think scares me is that I don't want to be *that* girl. The girl who thinks she's getting married and then the man runs away from her. And if I'm truthful, deep down in my heart, I wonder what will happen if we get close to marriage and then you do the same thing to me." She was being as honest with him as she possibly could.

"That would never happen, Tulip. I feel something for you in my heart that I've never felt for another girl—ever. Things are different with you."

"I'm scared."

He nodded. "I understand that, but I don't know what to do about it. All I can do is tell you how I feel and tell you that if my parents were forcing me to marry you, I would've gladly gone ahead with it."

She couldn't stop herself from smiling. "You would've?"

"Not only that, I would've told them to bring the wedding forward." He laughed. "I don't know why you're looking so surprised. I thought you knew how I felt about you."

"Not so much, but I'm glad I know now. It makes me feel better."

"Can we start where we left off? You agreed to be my girlfriend, remember?"

"I remember."

"Let's start from there and then when we get to know one another better I might let you marry me."

Tulip put her hand to her mouth and giggled. "If we married, I have to tell you now that I would never allow you to cook."

"Not fair. I like cooking. You can't prevent me from cooking over one incident."

"I can if that one incident nearly caused you to burn your *haus* down."

He laughed. "I guess that's fair enough. If you agree to marry me, I'll stay out of the kitchen."

"Good."

"So was that a yes?"

"A yes to what?"

"To marrying me?"

She stared into his eyes to see if he was serious. "Really?"

"I would marry you tomorrow if you said yes."

"We've not known each other for that long."

He took a step toward her. "We have a lifetime to discover things about one another. I tell you what, why don't you take as much time as you want to decide, knowing that you already have my heart. When you're ready, I'll be ready to marry you."

She wondered if he was making this grand gesture to

make her feel secure. If he was doing it for that reason, it had worked. All fear left her now that she knew how serious he was about her and their relationship. "Okay. I like that idea."

"Can I be so bold as to take up that invitation from the other night for dinner with your *familye* once your *vadder* recovers enough for visitors?"

"*Jah,* I'd like that. *Dat's* okay now."

"What about Wednesday night next week?"

"Perfect. I'll cook your favorite food."

"You remember?"

"*Jah,* of course I do."

TULIP TOOK an early shift on Wednesday so she could cook the dinner just the way Wilhem had said he liked it. The twins weren't teasing her as they helped, as she thought they would. They seemed intrigued by Wilhem and were asking all kinds of questions.

"So he's Jonathan's cousin?" Daisy asked.

"*Jah,* that's right."

"So *Dat* knows the *familye?*" Lily asked.

"I'm not sure, but he knows Jonathan's family."

"If you marry him, will you have to move away?" Lily asked.

That hadn't even occurred to Tulip. She'd only thought as far as marrying him and not what their life would be like afterward. He could very well expect her to move anywhere. The last thing she wanted was to move away from her family. He'd said he would work there for a few months, then what after that? What if he was the type of man who liked to move around, staying a few months here and a few months there? She couldn't live like that.

"Well?" Daisy asked since Tulip was taking time to answer Lily's question.

"To answer your question properly, Lily, that's something I don't know."

"Yeah, well, would you move away if he wanted you to?"

"Can we talk about something else? You're making me nervous."

"It's just that we don't want you to move away," Lily said.

"We'd miss you," Daisy added.

"I'd miss both of you too and I wouldn't want to move away, but if I was really in love with someone and married, we might have to move to find work or something."

When their mother came into the kitchen, the girls stopped talking.

"How's the dinner coming along?"

"Fine, *Mamm*. I thought you agreed to have a rest and let us do the cooking?"

"I was trying to have a rest and then I heard a lot of talk from the kitchen. It smells good."

"*Denke*," Tulip and Daisy said at the same time.

Their mother fixed her eyes on Daisy. "When our guest arrives, don't forget it was Tulip who did all this. All you did was help her."

"I know that. She did most of it."

"Good, and it needs to be perceived that way as well, with no confusion."

Tulip turned away from her mother before she burst out laughing. Her mother was so desperate to get her married off to a nice man that she thought Tulip was trying to woo him with her cooking. Her mother was so old-fashioned that way.

"I feel like I can never do anything right," Daisy said. "I'll be sure to tell him that *she* did it all and I did nothing to help. Would you be happy then, *Mamm?*"

"Don't be ridiculous. You're close to being sent to your room and having dinner up there as well."

"Sorry."

"Now, no more silliness. This is an important dinner for Tulip, so you can apologize to her as well."

Tulip felt sorry for Daisy, but not sorry enough to intervene and risk getting on the wrong side of their mother.

"Sorry, Tulip."

"That's okay."

Mamm said, "I'll sit back down with your *vadder* if I'm not needed in here."

Tulip said, "We're fine in here *denke, Mamm.*"

When their mother had left the room, Daisy shook her head. "What's wrong with her? She must've got out on the wrong side of bed this morning."

"She's nervous about dinner." Tulip opened the oven door and checked on the meat.

"Why should she be nervous about dinner? If anyone should be nervous it should be you."

"She wants to get me married off." The meat was perfectly done. She switched the oven off. "Now for the gravy."

"Can I do that? I love making gravy. And I'll pretend you did it."

"You don't have to pretend I made it. That's silly," Tulip said.

Daisy raised her fine, dark eyebrows. "Tell *Mamm* that."

"Oh, yeah." Tulip giggled. "Well, just don't say anything in front of Wilhem because you'll get into trouble."

The girls placed the roasted lamb and vegetables into a separate pot to keep them hot while Daisy made gravy from the pan juices.

Lily had just finished setting the table when they heard a buggy.

"This'll be him," Lily squawked.

"Don't look too excited," Daisy whispered. "Just play it cool."

Tulip hoped she hadn't made a big mistake by inviting him there. Then she remembered he'd invited himself. If things got really bad she'd remind him of that. He'd see the funny side. How bad could her family be to the man she was interested in? She would soon find out because she could hear her mother opening the front door.

"Go out and greet him," Lily quietly urged.

"I will. I'm just checking on a few things in here first."

"We'll look at everything in here. You go."

"Okay, I'm going." Tulip grabbed a hand towel, wiped her hands, and then headed out to see Wilhem.

By the time she got to the living room, he was sandwiched on the couch between her mother and her father, looking most uncomfortable. He looked up and smiled when he saw Tulip approaching him and gave her a nod.

She gave him a little wave and sat down to listen to what her mother was talking to him about.

"Well, Mrs. Yoder, I'm not totally certain how long I'll be here. I could stay longer depending on the job."

"Dinner is only going to be a couple of minutes away," Tulip said.

"Oh, Tulip. Look at what Wilhem brought me."

Tulip looked to where her mother pointed. There was a huge vase of flowers. He was certainly trying to win her mother over and it looked like it was working. "Oh, they look lovely and so colorful."

"It was so thoughtful. Every flower represents the name of each one of you girls—roses, tulips, lilies, and daisies."

Wilhem chuckled. "I couldn't come here empty-handed, Mrs. Yoder, not when you made all those lovely whoopie pies for Tulip and me the other night."

"Did you like them?"

"They were the best I've tasted."

"Nancy is a fine cook," Tulip's father told Wilhem. "Now, when I married her, she wasn't so good, but she's come a long way."

Nancy cackled. "We had a few mishaps along the way, but that was before I had a proper stove, Hezekiah."

Hezekiah teased his wife, saying, "Well, they say a poor workman blames his tools."

Nancy made *tsk tsk* sounds. "Don't listen to him, Wilhem."

Wilhem looked like he didn't know what to say, then after a few awkward seconds said, "The dinner smells *wunderbaar.*"

"Our Tulip cooks well," her mother said. "She's rearranged her work to cook this meal. She said that roasted lamb with vegetables and gravy is your favorite meal."

He looked over at Tulip and smiled. "I'm glad you remembered."

"And I think there will be enough crispy pieces for you." She told her mother and father, "He likes the meat well done on the outside."

"*Jah*, it's tasty like that," her father said to Wilhem.

"I should see how it's coming along." Tulip went into the kitchen and checked on everything. Then she whispered to each twin to act naturally around her guest and not say anything to embarrass her. They said they would. Tulip stepped back into the living room and told everyone the dinner was ready.

They all sat down at the table with Mr. Yoder at the head. Everyone bowed their heads to say their silent prayer of thanks for the food.

When Tulip opened her eyes, she noticed that the meat had already been sliced. That was something that their father used to do. Mrs. Yoder took Wilhem's plate and filled it with food. It was an odd thing for her mother to do, but it reinforced to Tulip that her mother approved of him.

Tulip barely had to do any talking because her mother and father chatted away to Wilhem quite happily. They asked him about people they knew from his community. That was fine but then they got onto what kind of work he was capable of doing and what he'd done in the past. At one point, Tulip nearly had to tell her parents that they sounded like they were interviewing him for a job. Then she realized they kind of were. They were interviewing him as a potential husband for her. Thankfully, the twins had just eaten dinner quietly while looking bored throughout. All Tulip wanted was to be alone with him.

When it came time for dessert, Tulip was pleased to leave the table. The twins helped by clearing the dishes and helping Tulip place the dessert of fruit salad, ice-cream, and cheesecake in the center of the table.

Once her father started to help himself to the food, Tulip noticed that Wilhem quickly did the same—a sign that he too thought it a little odd that Tulip's mother put food on his plate. Since Tulip couldn't get a word in edge-ways between her parents firing questions at Wilhem, she had time to notice these things. To think that she'd been worried about the twins making him feel uncomfortable! Wilhem was handling it all well, although his cheeks were getting a little rosy.

Her parents hadn't questioned Mark like that before he married Rose, but then again, Rose and Mark had grown up together and Wilhem was someone they'd met only recently.

Wilhem didn't wait long after dinner to thank everyone and say goodnight. He'd stayed for a cup of coffee and more talk in the living room—just long enough to be polite.

Tulip walked out to his buggy with him.

"I'm so sorry about all of that," Tulip said.

"About what?"

"The interrogation. Don't pretend you didn't notice. I saw you getting all hot and flustered."

He chuckled.

"Oh, and those flowers—you won *Mamm's* heart with the flowers."

"Good. I'm glad she liked them. I got them from your *schweschder* at the markets. I told her I was coming here and wanted to bring flowers."

"So having the four different flowers was Rose's idea?"

"Nee. I had the idea of getting her flowers to represent the four of her *dochders."*

Tulip giggled. "I think you passed the test."

"You think so?"

"Jah, I think *Mamm* wants to adopt you. She never puts food on people's plates like that. I didn't know what she was doing at first. She sometimes puts meat on plates for guests, but that's only when she's doing the same with everyone else."

"I like your parents."

They walked down the porch steps.

"Me too. You got off easy tonight. Usually the twins are talkative and out of control. I had to warn them not to embarrass me."

"You shouldn't have done that. It might have been entertaining."

Tulip giggled once more. "You don't think my parents were entertaining enough?"

"They were all right. It's only normal for them to want to know more about me. Do they know that we're … close?"

"Jah. They figured that out. *Denke* for coming tonight. I feel a little closer to you now that you've been here and survived dinner."

"I've passed the test, have I?" He reached for her hand and took it in his.

"Ten out of ten."

"Really? I've done well. How are you feeling now about the incident in my past?" They'd just reached the buggy and he turned to face her.

"It's not as though you got married."

"*Jah,* but you knew that the other day, yet it still bothered you."

"It doesn't any longer."

"I think it might bother you a little. It's hard to get over something that quickly. I could see it upset you."

"There are two different ways of looking at the situation and I was looking at it in the worst and most negative way." She shook her head. "It was silly of me."

"Your feelings aren't silly. You can't help the way you feel."

She was starting to like him more and more. It was as though she finally had someone of her very own. Someone who'd always be her special person and always be on her side no matter what. "That's nice of you to say."

"I'm not saying it to be nice. I want you to be sure about me and I don't want to pressure you into anything. I know I gave your parents the impression that I didn't know how long I'd be here for, but I can be here for as long as I want. There's permanent work available for me here if I want it."

"You'd stay on?"

He nodded. "*Jah.* I don't know how much to say to you because I don't want you to feel obligated to me. There's nothing worse than feeling trapped. I've decided to stay here because I want to build a future with you. There, I've said it." He leaned against his buggy, still holding onto her hand as they faced each other.

"Really?" Tulip licked her lips.

"*Jah,* but if you change your mind, I'll accept that. Don't think you have to be with me because I want to be with you." He picked up her other hand to hold it as well.

His words told her how much he liked her. They also showed her how he had felt when he'd felt obliged to marry someone his parents thought suitable.

He glanced over her shoulder at her house. "Tonight was special."

"It was a little tense and we hardly had time to say anything to each other."

"Tonight was for them—your parents. If they feel comfortable with me, maybe you'll trust me more. I'll never disappoint you, Tulip, and I'll never let you down."

As they stood there under the moon and the stars, Tulip knew what he said was true.

Six months later...

NANCY HAD MADE a new family rule since her husband's health scare six months ago and that was that they would all gather at her house on the first Saturday of every month for a *familye* dinner.

As the family sat down for one of their dinners, Wilhem, who had been invited to join them, spoke up. "I have an announcement to make tonight."

Mr. Yoder chuckled. "This will be an interesting dinner. I can't imagine what news there could be."

"I can," Daisy said.

Lily piped up. "I could take a good guess, too."

"Well, the sooner you make that announcement, the sooner we can say our thanks for the food," Trevor, the second oldest son, said.

Nancy looked around at her two sons and four daughters. They were all grown up and she had two lovely daughters-in-law, one granddaughter, and one wonderful son-in-law. She looked at her second oldest daughter and the man she'd been spending most of her spare time with, Wilhem. The two of them kept staring lovingly into each other's eyes and Nancy knew they were going to say they were going to marry.

Mr. Yoder cleared his throat. "We have Wilhem who wants to say something. Is there anyone else who wants to say something?"

Nancy knew that her husband was hoping that one of their sons, or maybe Rose, would tell them they were having a baby. Looking at them now, Nancy knew that they had no such news. Her eyes drifted to young Shirley in the highchair. She'd have to be the only one for a while yet, it seemed.

Everyone looked at Wilhem. "Shall I say it now, or after dinner? Or maybe after we give thanks for the food?"

Tulip gave an embarrassed giggle.

Mr. Yoder said, "You can't make us wait any longer. Tell us what you've got to say."

Wilhem smiled and glanced at Tulip before he looked

at the others at the table. "Tulip has finally agreed to marry me."

"I knew it!" Daisy squealed.

"For real?" Lily asked.

Wilhem laughed. *"Jah,* for real."

Mrs. Yoder stood up and ran to hug Tulip and then Wilhem. Mr. Yoder and Tulip's brothers shook Wilhem's hand, while Tulip's sisters all got up to hug her. When everyone had congratulated the couple, they all sat back down.

"Well, I didn't expect that tonight," Mrs. Yoder said. "We'll have to start organizing everything tomorrow, Tulip. We'll go into town and buy material to make the dresses."

"Can Daisy and I be your attendants?" Lily asked Tulip.

"Of course you can. I want you both to be my attendants, if you'll behave."

"What do you mean, Tulip? We always behave."

Tulip laughed. "We'll talk about that later."

"We should give thanks before this food gets cold," Peter said.

"Jah, we should," Mr. Yoder said.

They all closed their eyes and each gave their silent prayer of thanks for the food.

As everyone finished, they began to help themselves to the food in the center of the table. Except for young Shirley, who'd been happily mushing cooked vegetables onto the plate while managing to get some of them into her mouth.

The twins talked excitedly between themselves about

what color their dresses would be and how they wanted them, while Nancy's daughters-in-law and Rose gave Tulip wedding advice.

WHEN THE DINNER was done and Wilhem was ready to leave, Tulip walked outside with him to say goodbye.

"I think that went well," he whispered as he leaned against his buggy. "Your *mudder* didn't cry, and your *vadder* didn't have another heart attack."

Tulip giggled and put her head on his shoulder. "They like you."

"The twins are excited."

"It's hard to tell. They're like that about most things." Tulip shivered. "It's cold."

Wilhem put his arms around her and held her close. "I can't wait until we're married and we can start our life together."

"Me too. I've never been happier." Tulip was pleased that they had taken the time to get to know each other and hadn't rushed into anything. Without a doubt, she knew that he was the man for her.

"I must go. I've got an early start tomorrow. Go inside; it's cold." He leaned down and kissed her cheek. "I love you, Tulip."

"I love you too," she whispered back.

Wilhem climbed into his buggy and turned the horse around, and Tulip watched as he headed back down the driveway. She looked forward to the time when they could live together as man and wife. When a chilling gust of wind swept over her, she hurried back into the house.

To Tulip's surprise, the twins had ordered their parents to relax in the lounge room while they cleaned the kitchen and did the washing up. Tulip stayed in the kitchen helping the twins.

NANCY WAS PLEASED that everyone in their family seemed to have their life in good order.

"I don't think I can take any more happiness," Nancy said, as she held Hezekiah's hand. "I'm glad that Tulip will marry Wilhem; I really like him."

He leaned closer and whispered, "You weren't so certain about Mark at the start."

"I was sure he was a good man, but I wasn't convinced that he was a match for Rose, but he was. Look how happy they are now."

Hezekiah nodded. "They've all made *gut* choices."

"I'm worried about the twins. I think we'll have problems with those two."

Hezekiah chuckled. "I think you worry too much."

CHAPTER 26

*T*ulip stood next to Wilhem as they were pronounced man and wife. She'd waited for this day for months. Wilhem took her hand and gave her a quick kiss on the cheek and together they walked out of Tulip's parents' house. It was the second wedding held there, the first being Rose's.

When Tulip stepped outside, she felt good in the blue dress her mother had sewn for her. She'd wanted to make it herself, but had given in to her mother's wishes and instead she'd helped the twins sew their dark green dresses. The twins hadn't been too happy about wearing that shade, but Tulip considered that it suited their coloring the best.

"We're finally married," he whispered to her as they walked over to the main wedding-breakfast table.

As the twins' giggles rang out close behind her, she said, "I'm glad."

"I hope I make you happy, Tulip."

"You already have, and you will."

He smiled and when they reached the table, he pulled out her chair for her. She sat down, and reminded herself to remember every single moment of the day. When Wilhem sat beside her, she looked across to the house to see her father step through the doorway. Tulip silently thanked God that He had spared her father from the close call he'd had many months ago. Her father was there to see her get married, and for that she was grateful.

After a minor squabble about who was going to sit beside her, the twins took their places next to her. Either Daisy won, or Lily forfeited, Tulip wasn't certain; all she knew was that Daisy sat closest to her and then Lily sat next to Daisy. Compared to their usual behavior, they were conducting themselves as mature young ladies. Tulip was proud of them for making the effort. Two of Wilhem's older married brothers sat on the other side of him.

Jonathon had moved back in with his parents to save money and, after this wedding, Tulip was certain that he and Chelsea would announce their wedding soon. She guessed that was why Jonathon had made the move. The house that Jonathon and Wilhem had shared would become the first house Tulip and Wilhem lived in as man and wife.

It felt strange to Tulip that she was on the other side of the wedding table this time and not running around helping with the food. This was one wedding she wanted her mother to enjoy. She had asked her mother to sit close to her and leave everything up to the other ladies, just this once.

· · ·

Nancy looked at her second-oldest daughter sitting next to her new husband, and leaned into Hezekiah. "Do you feel old? Most of our *kinner* are married and we only have two to go."

He laughed. "You make it sound like some kind of game when you say 'two to go.' Like you're hitting balls and you've only the remaining two."

"*Nee,* I didn't mean it like that. Now that we're only going to have the twins at home, I want them to stay for a few more years."

"They'll work things out for themselves. If you've found out something, Nancy, it should be that no matter what you do or say, you have little influence over them when they become adults. And that's the way it should be. We bring them up as well as we can, and then we must trust that their values are sound."

"*Jah,*" Nancy said, turning slightly to stare at her three daughters sitting at the wedding table, and then looking around for the remainder of her grown up children. "It's hard for a *mudder* to let them go, but at the same time, I want them to marry early so they have the best choice. The twins are already drawing close to their next birthday and if they wait too long …"

"They'll miss out," Hezekiah finished the sentence for her.

"I know you think I'm silly, but …"

"*Gott* needs people's actions to fulfil His will."

Nancy's mouth fell open. "How did you know I was going to say that?"

He shook his head. "And you think that the Lord needs your help to fulfil His plans?"

"It sounds silly when you say it." Nancy chortled.

"You've got one wedding where you can sit down and enjoy yourself. You're always so busy running here and there doing things for people. Do you think the world would stop if *you* stopped?"

Nancy stared into her husband's wise eyes and realized that she had been carrying many burdens.

He took hold of her hand. "Why do you think Tulip asked you to sit down for the meal rather than be in the kitchen? She wants you to share the enjoyment of today. And I want you to slow down and stop thinking of so many different things. The world will keep going without you being like an ox pulling the plow alone."

"I'm just trying to be helpful."

He squeezed her hand. "The time has come for you to be helpful to yourself and you might just find that things will work out the same without you. Maybe it's time to give others opportunities to be more helpful."

"That doesn't sound nice."

"You know what I mean."

She gave a little giggle. "All I can do is try."

"That's all I ask."

Nancy looked around her. There were some young men visiting that she hadn't met before and they looked about the right age for the twins. Her eyes were drawn to a particular young man because he was looking in one direction only. She glanced over her shoulder at the twins to work out which one he was staring at.

"Nancy, what did I just say?" Hezekiah asked her.

She narrowed her eyes and studied him for a moment. It was as though he knew what she'd been thinking.

When she opened her mouth to say something in her own defence, he said, "I know what you think before you do, and I know what you'll say before you say it. Just now, you were looking around for husbands for the twins, weren't you?"

She sighed. She'd been caught out.

He rubbed his knuckles against the beard on his chin. "Did you listen to a word I said just now? Let things follow their natural course like …"

"Like a boat sailing down the river?" Nancy tried to hold in her laughter. Hezekiah was always likening things in life to traveling down a river or a stream in a boat—mostly a sailboat. "You see, I know you pretty well too."

Hezekiah shook his head at her. Nancy leaned forward and when she had a quick look around and saw no one was looking, she gave her husband a kiss on his cheek. He smiled and Nancy knew that he knew she was going to continue doing what she'd always done. And she knew that he wouldn't mind.

THE NEXT BOOK IN THE SERIES

In the next book, Daisy is convinced she has found the man she will marry, but will this new man cause a falling out between the Amish twin sisters?
Book 3 Amish Daisy

A NOTE FROM SAMANTHA

I hope you enjoyed Amish Tulip and the happy ending.
Nancy, the matchmaking mother, is now worried about
the twins. Who could blame her?

It's often said that the order of the children in a family
have an influence on their personalities. The twins are in
the middle and have escaped the responsibilities the older
ones had. Will their immature ways lead them to make
silly choices regarding men?

I've loved spending time in the world of the Yoder family.

Samantha P

www.SamanthaPriceAuthor.com

AMISH LOVE BLOOMS

Book 1 Amish Rose

Book 2 Amish Tulip

Book 3 Amish Daisy

Book 4 Amish Lily

Book 5 Amish Violet

Book 6 Amish Willow

Box Set Volume 1
Contains books 1 - 3

Box Set Volume 2
Contains books 4 - 6